Business, Lianne reminded herself as he led her to the dance floor.

But how could she think about that when Ryan had his arm wrapped around her? He shifted the hand he held around her waist.

"You okay?" he asked.

She had come here tonight to show him—and everyone—how well she could handle herself. How could she let him think she couldn't manage something as simple as a dance?

"No problem," she said, looking down, using the sight of his broad, solid chest to help her focus.

His fingers moved restlessly at the small of her back. Slowly, she raised her gaze.

He smiled.

She had no control over the way her heart fluttered at that moment. She wanted him to smile that way again, for her alone.

But if he did, she would never be able to resist... anything.

Business. She closed her eyes, took a deep breath and inhaled the delicious scent of his aftershave.

Ryan stopped moving. Lianne opened her eyes and glanced up at him. He was smiling down at her again.

Business...or pleasure?

Dear Reader,

With every book I write, I'm like a proud mama wanting to tell you how wonderful and special the hero and heroine are and how much they deserve their happy ending. That has never been more true for me than with this story.

Despair over a family tragedy has left Ryan within inches of losing his job, his reputation and his self-worth. All he has—all he is—rides on one last chance for redemption...but there's one woman standing in his way.

As a deaf woman caught between two cultures, Lianne has faced challenges throughout her life. When she's blindsided by someone she trusts, she's determined to prove herself—even though it means rebelling against her new boss.

With a little help from the folks of Flagman's Folly, these two people who are absolutely wrong for each other could make a perfect match. But first, they'd have to let down their guards. Are they willing to take the risk? I hope you enjoy finding out!

I love to hear from readers. You can reach me at P.O. Box 504, Gilbert, AZ 85299, or through my website: www.barbarawhitedaille.com. I'm also on Facebook: www.facebook.com/barbarawhitedaille and Twitter: twitter.com/BarbaraWDaille.

All my best to you,

Barbara White Daille

RANCHER AT RISK

—

BARBARA WHITE DAILLE

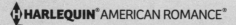

HARLEQUIN® AMERICAN ROMANCE®

Recycling programs
for this product may
not exist in your area.

ISBN-13: 978-0-373-75505-9

RANCHER AT RISK

Copyright © 2014 by Barbara White-Rayczek

Printed in U.S.A.

ABOUT THE AUTHOR

Barbara White Daille lives with her husband in the sunny Southwest, where they don't mind the lizards in their front yard but could do without the scorpions in the bathroom.

A writer from the age of nine and a novelist since eighth grade, Barbara is now an award-winning author with a number of novels to her credit.

When she was very young, Barbara learned from her mom about the storytelling magic in books—and she's been hooked ever since. She hopes you will enjoy reading her books and will find your own magic in them!

She'd also love to have you drop by and visit with her at her website, www.barbarawhitedaille.com.

Books by Barbara White Daille

HARLEQUIN AMERICAN ROMANCE

1131—THE SHERIFF'S SON
1140—COURT ME, COWBOY
1328—FAMILY MATTERS
1353—A RANCHER'S PRIDE
1391—THE RODEO MAN'S DAUGHTER
1416—HONORABLE RANCHER

To anyone who steps to the music
of a different drummer.
I hope that's you!
And, as always, to Rich.

Chapter One

"I'm sending you to the ranch in New Mexico."

Nothing like condemning a man without a fair trial.

Somehow Ryan Molloy managed to keep from saying that to the man standing in the barn doorway. What did it matter, anyway? Trial or no trial, he'd already condemned himself. His gut-level response at hearing his boss's words only piled on the guilt.

"Plan on being there by the end of the week."

Keeping a stranglehold on the reins in his hand, he nodded.

Over the past few months, Caleb Cantrell had allowed him more than a few chances to pull himself together and get his life back on track. No need for Caleb to voice *his* thoughts. The fact that he'd made the day trip from New Mexico to Montana said it all.

As if reading his mind, Caleb said, "I don't reckon I need to state the obvious."

"That I've given you no choice?" Caleb wasn't giving him one, either. No option of staying on the ranch here in Montana. He could take the offer. Or walk.

Raising no argument, asking no questions, he returned the reins to their peg on the wall, making sure they hung neatly in their appropriate spot. Too bad he hadn't handled things with such care earlier in the week.

As if in tune with his thoughts again, Caleb said, "What happened with Rod?"

"You haven't heard?"

"I want to hear it from you."

He shrugged. "He mouthed off about folks—about the manager—not attending to business around here."

Caleb frowned. "He didn't come across that way when we hired him."

"He was drunker than a skunk the other day," Ryan admitted.

"He didn't mention that."

"Why would he? Doesn't matter. He was in the right. And I did the unthinkable." Let months of anger and frustration and plain raw pain get the best of him. He forced his hands to relax by his sides. "I threw a sucker punch at one of my men. And you're relocating me to the new ranch." His own actions had led to this, yet the words left a bitter taste against his back teeth.

Caleb nodded. "For the time being. I need someone in Flagman's Folly, and you could use a change of scenery."

And a change in attitude.

More words he and the boss didn't need to have out in the open between them. He heard them loud and all too clear.

He heard them ringing in his ears even now, though that conversation had taken place days ago. Afterward Caleb had hustled off to the airport, but not before Ryan assured him he would see him in a few days.

In the weak morning light of his ranch-house bedroom, Ryan fumbled in his dresser drawers, scooping up the items he would need for a temporary but indefinite stay and shoving them into the duffel bag on the bed.

T-shirts…handkerchiefs…briefs…bandannas… And heck, why not take the Louis L'Amour paperback from the nightstand, too? The slip of paper marking his place in the book had rested between pages eight and nine for only about six months. He just couldn't seem to focus on the damned story, no matter that over the years he'd read it so many times he had practically memorized every word.

He managed to ignore the dresser top and the picture frame he'd turned facedown a year ago. He could stand beside a rectangle of freshly turned soil, could stare at names and dates on a chiseled stone, but he hadn't the willpower to look at that photo.

Again he swallowed against the bitterness threatening his molars. Leaving Montana meant walking away from every connection he had to Jan and Billy. It meant running away from the memories, too, the good ones he could barely recall anymore, blotted out by the bad ones he couldn't forget.

A year since the accident, those memories still filled his days and occasionally woke him in the dead of night. The pity in his friends' faces had added a few more rips to the torn-up places inside him. And last week, a drunken cowboy's insults had pushed him to his breaking point.

His throat tightened. Despite the breeze blowing in through the open window beside the bed, sweat dotted his brow. Hands hovering above the duffel bag, he paused. Before he could argue or talk himself out of his action, could brush away or second-guess the thought, he grabbed the picture frame from the dresser and slid it, still facedown, under a pile of shirts in the bag.

He would head out late afternoon, once he'd taken care of his chores here on the ranch one last time. Once he'd swung by for a last visit to the small churchyard on Hanaman Road.

And then...

Then he'd drive to New Mexico.

Only a fool would pass up the opportunity Caleb had given him, one he'd done less than nothing to deserve.

Somehow he had to undo the damage he'd done, to restore his credibility with the boss. To earn back his reputation.

The hell of it was, most of him didn't give a damn about all that. The wonder was, a small part of him still cared enough to fight for it. Plain enough to see the unexpected reassignment would be a battle.

A trial.

A risk he couldn't afford not to take.

ONLY A SHORT while into his solo journey, one stretch of road had started looking like any other. He drove through the night, when all the towns he came to had rolled up their sidewalks and gone to bed. Or—in the case of his arrival in Flagman's Folly, New Mexico, sixteen hours later—hadn't yet unrolled those sidewalks to a new day.

As he turned onto Signal Street, he figured he could describe the main thoroughfare with his eyes closed; it was almost exactly like all the other main streets in every other small town. Some stroke of luck—*good* luck, for a change—made sure his eyes stayed open. Up ahead of his pickup truck, a little girl darted into the roadway.

The luck stayed with him, letting reflexes take over. Lungs sucked in a breath. Ribs strained. Arms jerked in tandem with his wrench of the steering wheel, and both legs joined forces to jam the brake. Momentum hurled him against the shoulder belt and then ricocheted him back into the driver's seat.

Far past the end of the truck's high hood, the little girl turned around, met his eyes through the windshield and gave him an angelic smile.

As he sat there shaking his head and willing his heart to beat again, the air left his lungs in a whoosh. Other reactions washed through him, no less powerful for the delay. A tremor that shook him from head to toe. And an immediate understanding of something he'd never before believed—in moments of extreme stress, life *did* flash before your eyes.

Not only your own life but those of people you loved.

In the street, a slim woman hurried over to the girl. A puppy bounded across the adjacent lawn to join them and looked up, tail wagging and head cocked as if to ask what had happened.

The woman led the child back to the sidewalk—where she should've stayed all along. What if—?

He swallowed hard, unable to finish the sentence, even in his mind. Only moments ago he'd shoved a slew of year-old questions like that from his thoughts. Now he could barely think at all.

Both hands scrabbling, he unclasped his seat belt and shoved the door open. As his feet hit the ground, he nearly choked on the smell of scorched tires. A burning sensation raced through his insides. Pain-fueled anger flared. "Lady," he shouted, "are you crazy?"

Even from several yards away, he saw her blue eyes narrow. She spoke, but he couldn't catch the response.

Again he shook his head, wanting to chase away the memories triggered by the near miss. Needing to focus on the here and now.

She said something else, and still he couldn't make out the words. Obviously she was wrought up, with good reason. But that didn't account for the blurriness of her voice.

The hairs on the back of his neck rose. She'd risked her little girl's life.... "Are you drunk?" he demanded.

"No, I am not." She clipped off each word now, making a visible effort to speak calmly and clearly.

He frowned. Whether she denied it or not, something was up with her. "What the hell were you thinking, letting that kid run into the road?"

"I didn't let her. She chased after her puppy, and it was too late for me to stop her."

Too late.

Not, thank God, for this little girl.

"I'm sorry," she said in a softer tone.

He could hear the ring of sincerity, but couldn't shake off the visions of her child. Or his own. Under his breath he muttered what he'd been forced to learn: "Being sorry won't save your kid."

"I told you, it happened too fast."

He blinked, willing to swear he hadn't spoken loudly enough for her to hear.

Ignoring him, she turned to talk to the girl.

With neither of them paying him any mind, he sagged against the sun-warmed metal of the truck and scrubbed his hand across his mouth, glad for the chance to pull himself together.

He still couldn't shake the images that had peppered his brain like buckshot the moment he'd seen the girl run into the street. He couldn't stop the questions he had hoped to leave a thousand miles behind him.

Had memories flooded Jan's mind in the seconds before the crash? From his booster chair in the backseat, had Billy seen the end coming, too?

From somewhere deep inside, he found the strength to slam a mental door shut on his thoughts. For now.

Avoiding the pair on the sidewalk, he stared down the length of the street, taking in the general store, the pharmacy and a café. When he could breathe regularly again, he checked out the lawn alongside him. The town green, evidently, judging by the formal look of the hitching posts spaced all around the property and the horse troughs overflowing with flowers decorating the walkway. It almost seemed like home.

Good thing he'd never been here before, because this would've been one hell of a homecoming.

And good thing he didn't intend to stay long. Didn't matter what his boss said about "fresh starts" and "taking a breather." No one here but Caleb's wife, Tess, and daughter, Nate, knew him, anyway. But even that didn't matter. He would do his job, make things right with the man who paid his wages and move on to…who the hell cared where.

Trying to ignore the sudden stiffness in his shoulders, he focused on the building ahead of him. Tall columns held up the porch, though the structure looked sturdy enough to do without them. Beneath that sheltering roof stood a white-haired man impersonating an Elvis gone forty years past his prime.

Great. If he'd had to ruin his grand entrance, couldn't he have done it without an audience? The irony made his shoulders grow even more rigid. A year ago he'd hounded the sheriff's office to come up with a single witness.

Maybe the way the old man stood squinting and patting his shirt pocket meant he couldn't see a thing without glasses.

Naturally, all his good luck had run out. Elvis pulled a toothpick out of that pocket, stuck it in the corner of his mouth and crossed his arms over his chest. The old guy looked him up and down much the way Ryan himself inspected potential ranch stock.

Yeah, just great.

Distracted by movement, he looked toward the woman, who had turned to face him again.

A heavy feeling started in his chest and only got worse when she stalked toward him. Slim legs in below-the-knee shorts flashed gracefully but with as much determination as a filly headed for the finish line. He barely had time to take in the rest of her racehorse-lean frame before she came to a stop a yard from him. Her cheeks flushed pink with anger and her blue eyes flamed.

"I explained to Becky what happened," she said, spacing her words, "and now I'll explain some things to you." She spread the fingers of one hand and ticked off each statement as she made it. "I am not drunk. I am not crazy. Becky is not my child."

He shifted his shoulders again. She had a heck of a lot of points to get across, all on his account.

Beyond her he saw the little girl, as blond-haired as the woman in front of him. No wonder he'd taken them for mother and daughter. The child went onto one knee to pet the puppy.

"Becky is my niece. And—" the woman tapped her final finger, then curled both hands into fists and slammed them down in front of her "—I *can* take care of her."

The sparks in her blue eyes made him fight not to wince. She had some justification for her anger. He wouldn't deny that. He had good reason for getting upset, too.

But he didn't have enough damn fingers for his list of regrets.

Yeah, at first fear had driven him. Once he saw the child was okay, relief had set in. But then, as with the drunken cowboy, he had let frustration take over.

He couldn't lose it with her again.

"Look," he said, "when I saw the girl, I thought—"

"We've covered what you thought."

"Right. And you've said a mouthful about it. Or maybe a handful." He gestured to her fists.

She looked down. Again she made a visible effort to gain control, to unclench her fingers and let her hands hang naturally by her sides. He ought to take notes.

When she met his eyes again, he gave her an unblinking stare.

"I've already apologized." She spoke softly, indistinctly again, making him strain to focus on her words. "I'll say it one more time. I'm sorry Becky ran into the road and gave you such a scare. But she wasn't anywhere near you. You just overreacted."

Another truth he couldn't deny. No matter his unease about the woman, she was right. He *had* gone over the top with his reaction. The child had run into the road dozens of yards away from the truck, and he'd had plenty of time to come to a stop. Yet if he'd been closer to her, if he'd been distracted, if a car had come from the other direction... Too damned many ifs.

"You should have called her back," he said flatly.

"She wouldn't have heard me. She's deaf."

"Deaf?" He shifted his shoulders, trying to shake off the extra guilt her statement had added to him. He'd really messed things up today. Earlier this week. In the past few months.

Once, he'd listened to folks instead of jumping to snap decisions. It made him a better ranch foreman. A better man. *Once.* And now? He took a deep breath and let it out. "Look, I'm sorry—"

"Because she's deaf."

"No—"

"Because you realize you shouldn't have made assumptions about me."

"I wouldn't do that."

"You already did, didn't you? Why else would you have asked if I was drunk?" Her words now came through to him loud and clear. Her irritation practically rang in his head.

So much for attempting to save the situation.

Frustration clawed at him, yet guilt weighed him down. As fast as everything had happened, as incensed as he had been, he *had* jumped to conclusions about her. Keeping his tone as level as he could, he said, "You're jumping to a few conclusions about what I'm trying to say, too."

When he pushed away from the side of the truck, bringing them closer, she tilted her head back, keeping their gazes locked. "If you hadn't kept making your points and cutting me off, by now I'd have told you I'm sorry this whole thing happened."

She blinked and stared at him for a long moment. "Well," she said finally, "in that case, I guess we've both said all we needed to say."

He watched her turn and motion to the girl, who fell into step, her hands moving, as they walked away.

The dog sat on his haunches, wagged his tail and looked at him.

A good part Labrador with some shepherd in his bloodline, the pup had a dark coat but a tan-colored face. Dark fur circled one eye as though he stood staring with an eyebrow raised in question.

In answer, Ryan shrugged.

The dog whined, his thoughts plain enough to read. *Us guys ought to stick together.* Tail drooping now, the pup turned and padded after the pair of females who'd left him behind.

Could things get any worse?

"Ahem."

Startled, he turned to find the man had come down from the porch and moved to his side. Not good, letting himself get so distracted he'd given Elvis a chance to sneak up on him.

"I reckon that wasn't the best way to start off," the man said with a strong Texas twang. The woman's blue eyes had flamed in irritation. The old man's, a lighter shade of blue, seemed to bore right into him. And judging by his expression, the guy didn't much care for what he saw.

Ryan faced him head-on, widened his stance and crossed his arms.

"Around these parts," the man added, "folks respond better to kind words than to being called crazy." He shifted the toothpick from one side of his mouth to the other. "You'd best remember that if you plan on staying here for long."

"What makes you think I'm staying?" he asked, genuinely curious. "Maybe I'm passing through."

The man shook his head. "We're too far from the interstate for sensible folks to detour through town. And we don't get a lot of drop-ins all the way from Montana."

Frowning, Ryan shot a look at the dirt-covered pickup truck behind him. Considering they stood broadsides to the vehicle, the old man couldn't have seen the plate at the rear. "How did you figure out where I'm from?"

"Didn't have to figure a thing. People keep me informed. They know I like to stay on top of what goes on in *my* town."

Ryan stiffened. "*Your* town? Just who are you, if you don't mind my asking?"

"Don't mind a bit. Lloyd M. Baylor." As they shook hands, the man's eyes squinted with his smile. "Welcome to Flagman's Folly, Mr. Molloy."

Ryan froze with his arm still outstretched. He hadn't introduced himself. Instantly, he dropped his hand to his side, hoping the old man hadn't noticed the hesitation. Not much chance of that. Those blue eyes hadn't squinted from a smile after all but from a calculating stare.

Scrutinized like horseflesh once again—and passed over.

Just as when he'd spoken with the woman, his gut told him something wasn't right. But this time, he wouldn't jump to a response. Keeping his tone level, he said, "Have we met?"

"No, but I know all about you."

"From Caleb Cantrell?" So much for a fresh start.

The older man nodded as if he'd listened in on Ryan's thoughts. "Yep, heard all about you from Caleb. And there's no need to get up on your high horse about it. He and I go back a long way. He trusts me just like I'll trust you. If you don't give me cause to do otherwise."

"Is that so?"

"Yes. And I'll tell you something else. Flagman's Folly is the nicest place anyone would ever want to visit, including you. Just make sure you behave accordingly and keep out of my place of business."

The local saloon, Ryan surmised, judging by the man's string tie and red suspenders. He gritted his teeth and tried for a grin. And promised himself he wouldn't raise a glass in *that* barroom. "You're not living up to Caleb's talk about the town's friendly reputation, Mr. Baylor. If that's how you welcome newcomers, I'm surprised you have any customers at all."

"Customers?" The old man gave a gravelly laugh. "Never heard folks call it that, but I reckon the word works just as well as any other."

He frowned. "What kind of place are you running?"

The man jerked a thumb over his shoulder at the building behind him. "You're looking at it, son. This is Town Hall, and I run the courtroom." After eyeing Ryan for a long moment, he added, "You're more than welcome to stop by my office anytime. As long as you show up with a clean conscience and without a lawyer in tow." He nodded once to underscore his words before heading back along the trough-lined path.

Ryan clamped his jaw shut and shook his head over that so-called invitation. What had Caleb told the judge about him, anyhow?

Swearing under his breath, he climbed into the truck and slammed the door shut behind him.

He'd picked a hell of a way to make a first impression on folks in Flagman's Folly.

Chapter Two

A flash in the mirror above the dresser made Lianne Ward automatically turn toward the doorway of her temporary bedroom. Her sister lumbered into the room, both hands supporting her lower back.

"Here, sit down." Lianne swept aside the freshly washed clothes she had piled onto the bed. In the two days since her arrival, she hadn't had a single private moment with Kayla. If her good luck held until Becky came running into the room, maybe she could continue to avoid the conversation she didn't want to have. If not, she might as well wave a white flag and surrender.

Never argue with a pregnant woman, someone had once said. Great advice, especially with this pregnant woman, who never liked to take no for an answer.

Besides, Kayla could sign.

Sure enough, the minute their gazes met, she started in, using both hands and voice. *"You've been avoiding one-on-one time with me since you got here. What's up?"*

"Nothing."

"Come on, big sis. You don't expect me to believe that, do you?"

"You're the big one right now." What a relief to be able to tease Kayla, to say what she wanted without having to speak slowly, without focusing on each word and every syllable.

To talk without thinking about her voice at all. So different from this morning and her run-in with that impossible man who accused her of making assumptions about him. He'd done the same with her....

But didn't *everyone,* if not sooner than later?

She loosened her grip on the T-shirt she had intended to fold. If she didn't watch out, her own sister would start jumping to conclusions. She forced a smile. "It's only April. Are you sure that baby's going to wait another three months?"

Kayla was so lucky to have Sam and Becky and another child on the way. But even the mention of the baby didn't seem to distract her sister now.

Kayla rested her hand on Lianne's arm, the way she'd always done to get her full attention. *"The baby will come when he's ready. What I don't understand is why you're so ready to leave."*

"Miss me already? Don't worry, you'll have enough company when Sam's mom gets here."

"That's months away!"

"But if Sharleen hears I'm staying, she might start thinking she's not needed."

Kayla circled her right forefinger at her temple, making a sign that needed no words. Obviously, she hadn't fallen for Lianne's crazy excuses.

"You know I have to go," she said gently. "I made a commitment." And unlike some people, she stuck by her promises. "Besides, I'll only be a few miles down the road, close enough to come running as soon as Sam texts to let me know you're in labor. And I'll be by plenty of times before then. As you said, we've got months before the baby comes."

Kayla shook her head. *"What about Becky?"*

"She'll see plenty of me, too." She took great care in folding another shirt. This visit had been the best break from her troubles she could ever have asked for. The only down-

side to the past couple of days—other than this morning—
had been the many times Kayla had skewered her with a
sharp-eyed gaze.

Even now, she wasn't letting lack of eye contact deter
her. She put her hand on Lianne's arm again and pointed
to the bed.

"You don't give up, do you?" Sighing, she sank to the
edge of the mattress.

*"Not when there's something wrong. You know how
happy I am to have you here. But I want to know why you
left Chicago ahead of schedule. I'm guessing it's connected
to Mark, since you haven't mentioned him once."*

"Don't worry about him," she said lightly.

*"I'm not. I'm worried about you. And I'm not taking a
brush-off for an answer."*

She shifted on the mattress. Kayla would only be upset
to hear she now had no steady relationship, no permanent
job and not even a home to call her own. All because of a
confrontation she *hadn't* walked away from the way she
had fled from that stranger on Signal Street. "You've got
enough on your mind. You don't need to hear my problems."

*"Listen, big sis, haven't we always confided in each
other?"*

For most things, yes. Not this. On the other hand, she
recognized on her sister's face the same stubborn look she
often saw in her own mirror.

Sighing again, she said, "The long story short is, things
with Mark didn't work out."

Kayla's eyes, as blue as her own, shone with tears. *"I'm
sorry. I thought everything was going so well. You've been
with him longer than anyone else I can remember."*

"Two years, three months, eight days. But who's counting?" The relationship *had* lasted longer than most. So had
Mark's apparent acceptance that she was deaf. "He turned
out to be just like some of the other guys I've dated—the

ones who are so sure I can't manage without their help."
How many times had she heard that? "He put an extra spin
on things, though." She looked away and then made herself meet Kayla's eyes again. "He said I'll never survive
without him."

"That's ridiculous!"

Lianne had no trouble reading the next word on Kayla's
lips. She shook her head. "Yes, he is that. But watch your
mouth, little sis. Your son might be able to hear you."

They both laughed.

"Anyway, you called it right about Mark. So he's history." Kayla's expression told her she hadn't done a good job
of keeping her feelings from her tone. She shrugged. "It's
okay. I'll get over it." And she'd learn from it.

Someday.

She dropped the folded shirts into her canvas carryall.
"Enough about him. How's Becky?"

"She's fine." Kayla shook her head. *"Sam and I have
talked to her over and over about being careful when she's
chasing after Pirate. Five-year-olds forget. We'll keep talking to her."* She stopped signing briefly to squeeze Lianne's
hand. *"I told you, it wasn't your fault."*

"She moved so quickly—"

*"She does that to me all the time. It's scary. Believe me,
I know. But you said the driver didn't come close to her."*

"He didn't. That's what I tried to tell him."

She'd been upset over the situation, too. He hadn't cared
about that. Maybe hadn't even noticed, considering the way
he had almost staggered from the truck, his face pale and
his eyes wide.

A twinge of guilt made her wince. He had also tried to
apologize. Yet after getting the final words in, she had stalked
away.

Kayla frowned. *"Is there something you're not telling me?"*

"No. Becky wasn't—"

"I'm talking about you. And that man."

"Forget him." She planned to. One look into his stormy-green eyes and she had instinctively known he would bring her nothing but trouble. She didn't need any more trouble.

To her relief, Becky burst into the room and, already chattering away, ran up to Kayla.

Like any child her age, her niece walked around with a head full of never-ending questions. And like any inquisitive, active child, she forever wanted someone to talk to and play with. Happily, thanks to her mommy, Becky knew plenty of kids who signed.

A five-year-old without friends who could communicate with her found life lonely and isolating at times.

Adults didn't have it any easier.

Why hadn't she seen through Mark sooner?

You'll never survive without me.

Ridiculous, as Kayla had said.

She couldn't bring herself to tell Kayla the words he had flung as his parting shot.

With his mouth so contorted in anger, his face so filled with scorn, she'd had trouble reading his lips. Seeing her struggle, he had gone out of his way to speak slowly and deliberately. To make sure she got the message:

You'll never make it anywhere, Lianne.

She understood that, all right. And those words had made her cut her losses and leave him.

No matter what he thought, she could live in both the hearing *and* the deaf worlds. And she would fight any man who wouldn't treat her as his equal in either one of them.

BY LATE THAT AFTERNOON, Ryan and Caleb had inspected a good portion of the eastern boundary of the new ranch. The horses had no trouble getting them back home, which reminded him of the question Caleb had asked that morning. Did he have any trouble finding the ranch? He had given Caleb a firm negative. He'd had no problem at all making his way there.

If only that had been true about his trip through town. All day, he'd had a hard time keeping the incident out of his mind. But no way would he bring it up with the boss.

"We'll take care of some of that fencing during the week ahead," Caleb said, looking at his watch. "Let's call it a day."

"Sounds good to me." It had been a long afternoon after a longer trip, and with all he'd had to get done before leaving Montana, he hadn't closed his eyes for almost two days now. But lost sleep trailed at the end of his long list of troubles.

Tony, the gray-haired stable hand he'd met earlier, ambled out of the barn, his gait unsteady due to a bum leg and a built-up boot heel.

As they dismounted, Tony gestured to the horses. "I've got these."

Ryan held on to the reins, standard procedure on the Montana ranch. Except in an emergency, a rider took care of his own mount. To his surprise, Caleb handed over his reins and then nodded at him. Frowning, Ryan followed the unspoken order.

After the cowhand had led both horses into the depths of the barn, Caleb said, "Tony's an old buddy of mine. When I got back home again, I went to Amarillo to look him up. He'd run across a mean bull in rodeo years ago. Not everybody's as lucky as I was."

Lucky, hell. He knew why the boss had just leaned back against the barn door to give his leg muscles a rest. The former bull-riding champ had met a badass of his own and still stiffened up after a while in the saddle.

"Once Tony heard I was buying the ranch, he said he'd

been spending too much time on his butt and wanted something to do."

That explained the new procedure with the horses.

Just like his boss, always willing to help an old friend.

"As you saw," Caleb went on, "there's still plenty of work to do and men and horses and cattle to bring in before this turns into anything like the working ranch in Montana." He looked at him. "We'll need to go over some specifics."

Ryan nodded. The tour had gone fine. Too fine, maybe. As he'd learned the hard way all through life, good things might come in threes, but so did bad ones. After his run-ins that morning with the unnamed woman and the judge, he wondered what to expect from his talk with the boss.

Not once since his arrival had Caleb indicated either by word or by action any lack of trust in him. But if he didn't watch his step, he'd be pulling stable duty with Tony.

Judge Baylor's name hadn't come up, either. Not for the first time, he wondered why the boss had talked to the man about him.

"I'll have the laptop with me tomorrow," Caleb continued, "and we can run over the list of wranglers we've got on board as of now."

"Good. Always nice to know something about the men you're working with." No reason he shouldn't get along with those here. He'd always done just fine back home... until lately.

"I mentioned the renovations." Caleb gestured toward the bunkhouse. "The contractor's not done yet with the addition. Things will be a mess over there for a while, but since we don't have a full crew, that shouldn't be a problem. I want you to bunk down here at the house, anyway."

Puzzled, Ryan said, "You and the family haven't moved in yet?"

"No. We're keeping our rooms at the Whistlestop for

now. My mother-in-law has plenty available." His grimace told Ryan business hadn't picked up for the family-owned inn. "Anyhow, the bunkhouse is low on the priority list. I've had the contractor's men working on the cabins."

"Cabins?"

"Yeah. Phase two." Caleb eyed him for a long moment.

From inside the barn, metal clanged against metal. A horse nickered. Tony's soothing response reached them as a murmur, reminding him of the woman on Signal Street.

Caleb gave him a wry smile. "We're not up to speed yet, mostly because it took me a while to decide what I wanted to do with the property. I've finally figured it out. We'll eventually get this place running as a working ranch. But along with that, I'm setting up a school for disadvantaged boys."

Ryan shoved his hands into his back pockets and forced himself not to break eye contact. Hell, not to break into a sweat. He knew enough about his boss's history to understand his interest in folks who didn't have much to call their own. But Caleb knew *his* history, too. "You never mentioned kids."

"I am now."

He sucked in a breath. This wasn't part of their deal.

As if they'd actually agreed on his reassignment.

"We've got student applications coming in, and we're in the process of hiring. Officially, we won't open till August."

Four months from now. He would be long gone.

The contractors had left a sawhorse just outside the barn door. He settled on it and crossed his arms over his chest.

"I've brought in a project manager to handle the school setup," Caleb added. "Meanwhile, I'll be keeping a close eye on things."

Ryan frowned. Did he plan to keep an eagle eye on *him,* too? Or a squint-eyed gaze like the one the judge had given him earlier? And how many other surprises did the boss plan to throw at him? "I met a friend of yours on my way through town this morning."

He gave himself a mental kick for blurting the statement.

Before he could get himself in deeper, a vehicle screeched to a halt in the front of the house.

Caleb looked at his watch again and pushed himself upright. "Speaking of friends, here's another one of mine you'll get to meet. The new project manager."

Thankful for the reprieve, he walked across the yard, trying to get a handle on the same issues that had dogged him all year. Frustration over circumstances he had no ability to control. Overwhelming anger at unanswered questions.

He shook his head. In the few hours since he'd set foot in Flagman's Folly, he hadn't done much of what he'd come here to prove—that he was back to his calm, rational, clear-headed self. Back to the self he was before the accident. Back to being a man his boss could trust.

He wondered what kind of man Caleb would trust to manage a project as big as building a school. He turned the corner of the house and got his answer. Not a man after all.

The third bad thing of his day had just arrived.

He stared past Caleb at the woman he'd had the run-in with that morning.

Chapter Three

Would she never get away from the man?

She just couldn't shake him off. On Signal Street. In her thoughts. And now on the ranch. Just behind Caleb, the cowboy crossed the driveway toward her, striding with his thumbs hooked in his belt loops like some Old West villain wanting quick access to his guns. Well, if he wanted a shootout, she'd give him one. And if he thought that unblinking stare of his would send her packing, he'd have to think again.

Caleb made introductions. She regained her focus barely in time to read the cowboy's name from Caleb's lips.

"...Ryan Molloy."

She plastered her smile in place and nodded silently. No sense wasting the effort to speak to the man. She'd been there, done that earlier and had felt the consequences of it ever since.

Unlike this morning, he seemed done with her, too.

"We were just talking about you," Caleb said.

She stood straighter. "Were you?" Had he already learned what had happened on Signal Street? With Becky involved, of course, she'd had to tell Kayla. But had the darned cowboy already spread the news to her new boss?

If Caleb did know, he chose not to mention it right then. "Ryan's come down from the ranch in Montana. I was starting to fill him in on our plans."

And why did the cowboy need to know?

Taking a deep breath, she forced another smile.

"We've decided to call it a night," Caleb said. "And before I forget to tell you—" he glanced at them both but kept his face turned toward her "—Tess and Roselynn already plan to set places for you at the Whistlestop for Sunday dinner. And Nate's got a whole list of questions she's saved for Lianne." He looked at her. "Okay with you?"

"That sounds perfect." Half the truth, since the cowboy had been invited along, too. But she had loved Caleb's new extended family the minute she'd met them at Kayla and Sam's wedding more than a year ago. "I'm looking forward to seeing them again."

"Good. I'll be back in the morning, then. Ryan, help Lianne with her gear when you bring yours in. Then you'll both be set for the night."

The sudden blankness in the cowboy's face alerted her. She could read lips with the best of them, but no one caught one-hundred percent of a conversation, even after years of practice. She had missed something. Something he didn't like. *What?*

She watched Caleb carefully as she said, "We'll both be…"

"Set for the night." He laughed. "Maybe better said, for the duration. Ryan's moving in, too."

Instantly, she made her face as blank as the cowboy's. She'd had plenty of practice in that, too, and she couldn't let Caleb see her dismay. But right now the last thing she wanted was to share space with anyone. Especially Ryan Molloy.

"You okay with that?" Caleb asked. "If not, we can get you a room at the Whistlestop."

"No, I'm fine," she blurted. As much as she liked his family, she needed time alone. She would have even less chance of that in a bed-and-breakfast inn than she would have had at Kayla's. At least here she had only the cowboy around. She would stay far out of his way.

"And you?" Caleb asked Ryan.

"I don't have a problem with it."

As far as she could tell, he'd spoken quietly—no exaggerated mouth movements, no strained muscles in his neck. Yet standing so close to him, she could swear she felt a tiny vibration rumble through her.

Caleb nodded at her, and he and Ryan walked toward Caleb's pickup truck.

Eyes narrowed, she looked the cowboy over from his broad shoulders to tight-fitting jeans. When she realized she was staring, she hurried around the end of her Camry. The man was irritating and confrontational—and not worth her time.

Everything inside the trunk had shifted during her trip, and it took a few moments to work some tangled straps free. Ryan reached forward to grab another bag. She nearly jumped out of her shoes. Even wearing her hearing aids, she couldn't pick up footsteps. But people coming up from behind her never startled her. Her nerves must need time to regroup as much as she did.

He gestured at the car. "Riding a little low to the ground, isn't it?"

"It's packed."

He nodded. "Yeah, I can see that. You've got more in there than most folks manage to cram into the back of a pickup. Looks like you brought everything you own."

"I did," she snapped. Regret flooded her. Why hadn't she kept quiet? He didn't need to know anything about her personal life.

Ryan reached for another bag.

"I can do that," she said quickly.

He nodded. "I'll start on the boxes in the car."

"That's okay." When he turned to open a rear door, ignoring her, she managed to hold her temper in check. Barely. Surely he knew he needed to face her when he spoke. "Caleb said you have your own things to unload."

He looked at her and shrugged. "Two duffel bags and an extra pair of boots." One side of his mouth curved up. "From the looks of it, your stuff will take a lot longer to unload than mine. And I'm beat. I'd rather get this done before I run out of energy."

"I *can* handle this," she said.

"Hey, I recognize an order from the boss, even if you don't. And I don't slack off anytime, which means I'm sure not going to do it when he's still here."

Heat flooded her face. She turned around to look down the length of the driveway. Sure enough, Caleb had just begun to back his truck onto the road in front of the house. His truck with the engine that was loud enough to make her aids vibrate.

Wonderful. Earlier, she'd messed up reading Caleb's words, and now she'd completely missed the clue that would have told her he hadn't yet left.

From tiredness, that was all. Tiredness after the long drive from Chicago. Excitement over the new job. Frustration over dealing with this darned cowboy again. And…

…and fear.

Normally, she *could* handle anything that came her way. But every once in a while when she thought of the scope of this project, a small part of her worried she'd gotten in over her head.

She owed that to Mark, too.

Forcing a smile, she waved goodbye to Caleb. Then she turned back to Ryan, moments too late. He had pulled a box from the backseat of the Camry, taken the bag from the trunk, and was already going up the front porch steps.

The box he carried, filled with books and file folders, weighed a ton. Ryan cradled the cardboard box in one arm as though it weighed no more than the pillow she'd tossed on top of the bags in the passenger seat.

She stared at his arms and shoulders, at bulging muscles probably honed through hard labor. Nothing at all like most of the men she knew in Chicago, who sculpted their bodies at the gym. None of those men would have ventured out in public dressed the way he was, either, in boots so old and cracked that the leather had worn to suede in spots and jeans so threadbare they'd turned white in places. The perfect specimen of a true-blue, red-blooded, thank-you-ma'am-polite cowboy.

Until he'd started in on her this morning and the image had shattered like a mirror dropped on concrete.

Two HUNDRED YARDS shy of the railroad crossing at the south end of town, the car swerved, painting black rainbows on the asphalt, straightened again, slid forward and ended up grill-first against an unyielding concrete fence. Fiberglass popped. Distressed metal collapsed, twisting and bending, folding in on itself like a beer can in the hands of a drunken man.

He could smell the rubber, hear the metal scream, feel the pounding in his temples.

But he wasn't there....

He hadn't been there the day of the accident. He didn't know where he was now, other than sitting bolt upright in an inky darkness that stretched on into forever. His heart limped for a few beats as he sat waiting for his eyes to adjust.

Dead ahead a thin gold thread appeared, outlining a

dark rectangle—light seeping around the edges of a window shade. Off to one side of him, bright red LED numbers hovered in the dark like a candle flame. A bedside clock, reading 5:43 a.m.

The red images gave him his bearings: Caleb's ranch house, the guest room on the second floor, the faint light from the porch fixture outside. A deep sleep after two days of no shut-eye. A nightmare he had hoped he'd left behind.

The screeching metal and shattering glass had only added sound effects to a bad dream.

Then why did they still echo inside his head?

Lianne?

He crawled out of bed, grabbed his jeans and slid them on, all the while trying to identify the source and location of the racket that wasn't in his head at all. *And* that had just ended as abruptly as if someone had pulled a plug.

The noise had come from below.

He took the stairs in two leaps. Not a sound down here, and dark as pitch except for the band of light streaming from an open door halfway down the hall to the kitchen. The continuing silence made the previous noises all the more ominous.

He hurried toward the light from the office Caleb had shown him that afternoon and then skidded to a halt in the doorway, expecting splinters from the polished wooden floor to pierce his bare soles. One glance told him serious damage had been done.

Every door in the wall of custom-built cabinets hung wide open. A drawer of each file cabinet gaped. The rest of the room looked like a field back home after a winter storm, except instead of snow, every horizontal surface had been covered with clipboards, plastic filing trays and folders spilling their guts.

Over everything drifted the scent of freshly brewed coffee from a table in one corner, the only uncluttered space in the room.

In a far corner, his new housemate stood with her back to him near one of the file cabinets. She flung another folder the few feet over to the desk behind her without looking. It slid from the edge to join the rest of them on the floor.

What the—?

Maybe he hadn't woken up yet. He scrubbed his face with his bare hand, attempting to wipe away the last traces of drowsiness.

When he took his hand from his face, he found Lianne watching him.

"Couldn't sleep?" she asked.

Biting his tongue, he fought to come up with a question that didn't include any swear words. "What are you doing up?"

She shrugged. "I couldn't sleep, either. I've got a busy schedule, so I thought I would get in here and rearrange everything the way I want it. While I've still got the opportunity. Before I get to work."

She was babbling and, for the first time, had spoken to him naturally. Nerves had made her forget her defenses. Probably best not to point that out.

"Did you need something?" she asked.

"Some peace and quiet."

"Oh." She grimaced. "I forgot to close the door, didn't I?"

"You forgot more than that." He glanced at the center of the room. The sound of plastic file trays and a half dozen other items crashing to the floor in front of the desk had played right into the crumpling metal and breaking glass of his dream.

She followed his gaze. "I guess I got a little involved."

And a lot reckless.

Her cheeks pinker than the T-shirt she was wearing, she stooped and began scooping papers together.

He dropped to one knee and grabbed her wrist. When she looked up at him, her brows lowered, he gestured toward the floor. "Watch it. You'll hurt yourself."

"You're worried about paper cuts?"

"No. This." From under a flurry of paper, he lifted the jagged pieces of glass and wood.

She took the broken frame from his hand and turned it over. A trio of smiling faces looked up at them. Caleb. His wife, Tess. Their daughter, Nate.

"Oh, no. Caleb just had this photo taken." Lianne stared down, her face stricken. Broken glass had left a deep scratch across the surface.

"It's only a picture," he muttered. "Easy enough to replace."

She ignored him.

He took the frame from her and set it on the desk, then leaned over to start picking up files from the floor.

"Not those," she said.

He looked at her.

"They're in order. Organized chaos, I know. But that's the way I work."

"Right. How about I pick up what belongs on the desk and you take care of the rest?"

When he'd finished that, he rose and looked over at the coffeemaker.

"Want some?" she asked. "Help yourself."

"Might as well. I don't guess I'll be going back to sleep tonight." He looked at the pink-tinged sky through the office window and corrected himself. "This morning."

She picked up an empty mug from the desk. "Ranchers have to get up early, don't they?"

"Not this early," he said.

She flushed again but held out the mug. Once he'd filled it, she took a seat behind the desk. The power position.

"Maybe sharing this house isn't the best idea." Her gesture swept the room. "Obviously, I'm not the quietest person. I'd hate to interfere with your sleep again."

"I'm staying." As if he had a choice. "Once you're done fixing things up here, there won't be anything else to bother me. Unless you get hit in the middle of the night with an idea to rearrange heavy furniture."

"Very funny."

He sat on the small couch near the coffeemaker and stretched out his legs, crossing them at his bare ankles. Might as well make use of the time, too. Show Caleb he'd done his homework. "Tell me about the school."

She took a long deep breath followed by a sip of coffee. "Our overall mission is to provide a home for troubled boys. A residential school. They'll live here, attend classes and group therapy sessions, and have one-on-one meetings, as well."

He raised his brows. "Then you're talking behavioral counselors and teachers as well as camp counselors?"

"They'll be called aides, but they'll act as counselors like at a camp, yes. And only a small staff of teachers, since the older boys will take some of their classes online. We'll also have a live-in registered nurse."

"Sounds like a big operation."

"It will be. We're starting small and plan to increase enrollment in future." It was the most she'd said to him since their first meeting. She spoke slowly and clearly, ensuring he didn't miss a thing, as if she wanted to emphasize the importance of what she was saying. Or as if she recalled the conclusion he'd jumped to when they'd first met—that she was drunk.

At times, he still found her hard to understand, though even when he lost a few words along the way, he got the message. Considering her voice and her niece being deaf, he reckoned Lianne had some hearing loss, too.

"As part of the noncredit courses," she continued, "we'll teach life skills, rolled into lessons that fit with living on a ranch. Cookouts, hikes and nature walks, riding lessons. In fact, that part of the curriculum will run along the lines of a dude ranch. But don't tell Caleb's daughter that."

"Why not? When I met Nate at the ranch in Montana, she was all about horses."

"Oh, she still is. She's just not a fan of dudes." She gave a soft, throaty chuckle. "And she's not alone. When I first suggested Caleb turn this into a dude ranch, you should have heard the reactions of the people around here. It could have been a wise investment. But with the school, we've got so many more possibilities to make a difference." Her eyes shone.

When she wasn't glaring at him or counting off points on her fingers, she was a nice-looking woman.

What did that matter? He tightened his hand around the coffee mug. "And you're in charge of all this."

The light in her eyes dimmed. Her defenses had snapped back into place.

"I am." She said it flatly, as if expecting a challenge.

He'd give her one. "What makes you the right candidate for this job?"

"Don't worry about that. We'll have trained counselors to work with the boys. My role is strictly to take care of the behind-the-scenes operation."

"That's what I meant."

She stared him down. "I've got a B.A. in business administration and eight years' experience working with newly established companies."

He nodded. "Not in this area of the country, I take it, since you've made a move and brought everything with you."

"My sister, Kayla, lives here. She's married to one of the local ranchers. I'm from Chicago."

A city girl, then. Probably knew nothing about live critters except maybe for cats. "A boys' school doesn't exactly follow along the lines of one of your big-city corporations."

Her eyes narrowed. "What *exactly* are you saying?"

"For Caleb's sake, I hope you know something about dealing with kids." He gripped the mug again.

"I told you, my job is behind the scenes. And from here I do it all. Budgets, schedules, spreadsheets, insurance—" she gestured around the office again "—and whatever admin work needs to be done. And I have other experience that makes me qualified to deal with the boys. I'm sure they'll be much easier to work with than some men." She eyed him steadily.

No trouble catching any of that. Irritation had made her bite off every word.

"By the way," she said in the same clipped tones, "since you're determined to share the house, then we'll be taking turns with the meals." Over the rim of her mug, her eyes gleamed.

She thought she'd one-upped him.

He'd go her one better—though he knew the reaction he would get. "I don't cook." As she opened her mouth to protest, he added, "I'll take my meals with the ranch hands in the bunkhouse."

"That's fine with me."

"Right," he said under his breath.

"What?"

"Right. Glad we've got that settled. As for the rest—" he

looked around the room, then forced a smile "—I'm not a fan of organized chaos. You do your job, I'll do mine. And we'll stay out of each other's way."

Chapter Four

"The supply sheds still need to get stocked," Caleb said as he and Ryan stood in the horse barn, after their return from inspecting the western boundary. "The larger one first, since we'll start off grazing the herd near there."

Ryan nodded and made a mental note. "I'll add it to the list." He had spent the morning with Tony and a couple of the wranglers, hauling around all the new tack and equipment the boss had bought to outfit the barn. Close enough to the house that he could be ready to head out on his second tour with Caleb as soon as he was needed.

And far enough from the house to keep him out of range of Lianne.

Grimacing, his boss stretched. It was easy enough to see that another long afternoon in the saddle had him tired and sore.

"Getting to be an old man," Caleb said.

Ryan laughed.

"Aw, you don't know old," said Tony from his stool beside the mare he was grooming. By the look of him, he was pushing eighty.

"Well, I do know I'm ready to head for home." Caleb looked at Ryan. "You remember we're having dinner tomorrow?"

"It's number one on my list."

"Good. Tess and Nate are looking forward to seeing you again—"

Lianne had said the same about them.

"—and the ladies are eager to meet you."

"Are they?" How much had Caleb told them of his situation?

"Yeah." Caleb looked over at Tony. "Roselynn—Tess's mom—is a real Georgia peach. Roselynn's sister…" He grinned. "Let's just call Ellamae a chili pepper."

"She hot tempered?"

"No, she just likes to spice thing up."

Tony chuckled. "My kinda woman. I gotta meet her."

"I'm sure you will one of these days. She's bound to show up here to check things out."

After a couple of other reminders for Ryan's mental list, Caleb said his farewells. From the barn doorway, Ryan watched him head in the direction of the corral, where he had left his truck.

The back door of the ranch house opened, and Lianne stepped onto the porch. She called Caleb's name, then hurried across the yard to him, her blond hair streaming in the sun.

She moved like a thoroughbred. He'd noticed those long slim racehorse legs of hers right away. Well, after he'd gotten past the angry glare in her blue eyes.

Tony had come up to stand beside him. He gave an appreciative whistle. "Whoo. Speaking of women. She's a sight to behold, ain't she?"

Ryan shrugged. He'd looked at women, even all through his marriage—hell, he was a red-blooded male. But he hadn't often bothered to look twice.

He did want to work well with the men here. "She's not bad."

"Not bad?" Tony chuckled. "Boy, you must need glasses

more than I do. I can't hardly see the print in the newspaper anymore, but my long distance never lets me down. Even from here, I can tell she's easy on the eyes."

He had to agree.

They watched her leave Caleb beside the corral and make her way back to the house.

"Mmm-mmm," Tony murmured. "I haven't had the pleasure of meeting her yet, but I'm looking forward to that. Maybe I'll go chat her up sometime." His grin turned his face into a mass of wrinkles. "Like while you're off having your Sunday dinner with the folks."

"She's going, too."

Tony's face fell. "Well, dang. Now I'm disappointed Caleb didn't invite me along."

You can take my place.

A sentence Ryan surely wished he could say aloud.

Supper at the Whistlestop Inn might be all in a night's pleasure for the boss, but it was going to be work for him. A command performance at the least, if not a test to see how he could handle himself. So far Caleb hadn't put him in as manager. He hadn't said anything about his job.

When it came to aging, neither Caleb nor Tony knew the true meaning of the word.

He was the one getting old, fast.

RYAN MADE SHORT work of his shower and didn't waste any time getting dressed. Back in his room, halfway through straightening his cuffs, he stilled. It had been over a year since he'd dressed for a night out.

Only a week later, he had worn a plain long-sleeved white shirt like this one...with his dark suit....

One quick tug popped the snaps running down his chest. He pulled his arms free of the sleeves and shoved the shirt into his duffel bag. Whatever T-shirt he grabbed from the drawer would have to do.

At the dresser, he couldn't keep from looking at the picture frame pressed neatly against the beveled edge of the mirror. Safe. Secure. Still facedown.

He ran his comb through his damp hair, tucked the comb into his jeans pocket and left the bedroom. Maybe left the bad memories behind long enough to face the uncomfortable evening waiting ahead.

Halfway down the stairs, he jerked to a halt.

Lianne sat on the couch in the living room, her blond hair trailing down to the cell phone in her hands, her thumbs a blur as they flew over the keys. They'd gotten through the day without seeing each other, except to haggle over the shower.

She'd dressed up for the occasion. Flat red sandals, a brightly flowered skirt and a red blouse that was all fluffy and soft with lace edging.

The kind of thing Jan used to like.

Would the damn memories *ever* stop?

He couldn't speak, could only clear his throat, trying to get the woman's attention. Trying to get them moving and out of there so he could focus on the road and the drive into town and forget everything else.

She didn't look up or, as far as he could see, miss a beat from her texting. Ignoring him. No surprise.

He continued to the bottom of the stairs, wishing the quiet would last. Knowing with her around he didn't have a chance.

She slid her phone into a small red bag and stood. "All set?" he asked.

He held open the front door and then followed her out to the yard.

"We can go in my car," she announced. She stopped

and looked back at him, her hand on the driver's door of the Camry.

He shook his head. "I'll drive."

"I have a license, you know."

"I'm sure you do." He jerked his thumb toward his truck. "I need to gas up." As he turned away, he tried to lighten the statement. "Since I don't know where anything is, how about you ride shotgun."

"What?"

After a deep breath, he turned back. "Ride shotgun," he repeated. "It means—"

"I know what it means."

And she hated the idea. This was one heck of a spot Caleb had put him in....

He'd put himself in.

He winced. "Listen, I don't like the situation any more than you do. But there's no getting around it now. Unless you want to take Caleb up on his suggestion to stay at the Whistlestop." She lowered her head slightly to stare at him, reminding him of a headstrong mare he'd once known. "Okay, then. We'll be sharing quarters. And we can agree to disagree, if that's what you want. But things might run a whole lot smoother if we didn't argue every time we opened our mouths."

"I wasn't arguing with you," she snapped.

His turn. He stared her down.

"I didn't mean to yell." Now she kept her voice so soft and low, he could barely make out the words. "But I wasn't arguing. I just couldn't see what you said."

He frowned.

Her face froze. Slowly, her eyes widened. "I don't believe it. You don't know, do you?" She shook her head in wonder. "You haven't figured it out yet."

"Figured what out?"

"I'm deaf."

He opened his mouth and snapped his jaw closed again.

She stared at him, her eyes glinting in triumph the way they had when she had thought she'd one-upped him over taking turns with the meals.

Before he could respond, she opened the passenger door and climbed into the truck. He shook his head. Though he'd suspected she might have some hearing loss, it had never crossed his mind that she was deaf.

But she was right. He'd had enough clues to figure things out. She had jumped when he had walked up to help her unload her car. She hadn't heard that gigantic crash in the office. And she had stared at Caleb the entire time he had talked to her yesterday.

Sometimes she even gave *him* her attention when he spoke.

Through the rear window of the cab, he could see her waiting, seat belt in place over her shoulder. She hadn't wanted to ride in the truck, and now it looked as if nothing would get her out of it.

When he started the engine with a roar, habit had him reaching toward the dashboard. He froze, considered, then went ahead and turned the radio on. He always listened to the sports station.

A second later she reached out, too. Unlike him, she didn't hesitate. Instead, she hit the scanner till whatever number she'd searched for popped up. A hard-rock station, judging by the screech coming out of the speakers. Nothing could irritate him more.

He was wrong.

She wasn't finished.

She cranked up the volume till his ears rang and pushed the bass level to the max. He'd swear the danged windshield shivered. Clamping his jaw shut again, he rolled down his side window.

He fought not to look over at her. Why should he, when he already knew what he'd see? But to prove a point to himself for a change, he gave in and glanced across the cab.

Sure enough. Just what he'd expected. More sparkles in those big blue eyes and a wide smile on her pink mouth.

Again she thought she'd scored a mark on him.

Obviously, their situation meant only fun and games to her.

Let her play.

As he'd told her the other night, they both had jobs to do. And worrying about her didn't make it onto any of his lists.

ELLAMAE STOOD IN the middle of the kitchen at the Whistle-stop Inn and put her hands on her hips. The minute dinner was done, she and her sister, Roselynn, had had the good sense to shoo their guests and Nate out to the backyard.

Now the rest of them could get down to business.

"Ryan seems like a good man," she stated, checking faces to make sure no one disagreed with her judgment.

"He *is* a good man," Tess said.

Roselynn paused with the refrigerator door half-open. "Poor boy, he's had a bad time of it."

"Yeah," Ellamae said thoughtfully. "And he's due for a change."

She and the other two gals looked at the only man in the room.

Caleb held his hands up as if to ward them all off. "You'll get no argument from me, ladies. My point in bringing him down here is to give him a chance to pull himself together again. Whether he can do that or not, only time will tell."

"Time is just what he needs," Tess agreed.

"Being in a new environment will help," Roselynn said.

He nodded. "That's the whole idea."

"I can't imagine what he's going through." Tess rested her head against Caleb's shoulder.

"Not something I'd even want to consider." He wrapped his arm around her and pulled her close.

His jaw had hardened and his eyes had gone tight. Ellamae frowned, knowing what thoughts must've run through his head. Caleb had gone through hard times and come out a better man for it.

His ranch foreman would do the same, with luck—and a little help from Caleb's family.

When Tess and Caleb left the kitchen laden down with trays of mugs and the coffeepot, Ellamae glanced at her sister.

Roselynn looked back, her forehead wrinkled in concern. "He's upset over the whole situation, El, and who can blame him? I told him he did the right thing bringing Ryan here."

"Agreed," Ellamae said. "All along, it sounded like the boy was a powder keg sitting up in Montana, just waiting for a match to light his fuse. But I've got a feeling the distractions around here are going to take him right out of himself."

"I hope so. Although I don't see much difference between one ranch and another."

"It's not the job that's going to keep him—and us—busy."

"Oh, no." Roselynn shook her head. "Ellamae, he's still grieving."

"I didn't say we'd get busy immediately."

"You can't possibly be thinking of getting up to *anything.*"

She gripped the damp dishcloth she'd just used to clean the counter. "For crying out loud, woman. It's not me. Rose, sometimes, I swear you walk around with blinders on. You saw Lianne all through supper. Do you mean to tell me you didn't see the sparks from her flying across the table?"

"How do you figure that? She didn't say a word to him."

"I rest my case." She sighed. Sometimes Rose needed to be approached from a different angle. "Haven't we said all along Lianne's a wonderful girl?"

"Of course we have. And I want her to be as happy as Tess." Roselynn's face brightened. "What about Kayla and Sam's foreman? You know Jack's always been interested in her. And they get together whenever she comes to visit."

She waved the idea away. "He's a nice man but not good enough for Lianne."

"Well, I don't know...." Roselynn picked up the loaded dessert tray. "Ryan's just arrived in town. He hasn't even settled down yet."

"He won't get the chance to settle down." She laughed and tossed the dishcloth into the sink. "Trust me—" And why wouldn't anyone trust her, since she always knew what was what about everything? "—we'll be taking things nice and easy on this one. Give those two a little time on their own out at the ranch, and Lianne will have that boy well and truly riled up."

"We're having pecan pie," Nate said, spinning a couple of napkin-wrapped forks on the table. "Aunt El's best!"

Lianne smiled. Caleb's wife, Tess, was on the quiet side, while their preteen daughter was exactly the opposite. Nate reminded Lianne of herself at that age—a bit of a tomboy and always willing to take charge.

As guests, she and Ryan had been sent outside with Nate to sit at one of the picnic tables scattered across the Whistlestop's backyard. The girl hadn't stopped talking since they had left the house. A good thing, since Lianne wasn't sure she wanted to be left alone with Ryan.

"Gram's bringing the pie." Nate looked at him. "Aunt El wouldn't let me carry your piece because she said I'd snitch some of your pecans. But I wouldn't do that. Not the first time, anyhow."

All through dinner, Lianne had managed to keep up with the conversations—except when they involved much input from Nate. When she was excited, which was often, she talked right over others. Her exuberance, combined with how fast she spoke, made lipreading next to impossible.

She gave Nate a lot of credit for wanting to learn how to communicate with her and Becky, especially because many people never made the attempt. But now, as the girl moved on to tell Ryan a long story about a rodeo, she seemed to have forgotten she knew a single sign.

Lianne looked away, giving her eyes a rest. She made sure to keep her gaze from going anywhere near Ryan.

On their ride to the inn, he had done the same.

In the truck, she'd noticed he had shaved after his shower, closely enough for her to see the small muscle tic in his otherwise smooth jaw. She knew what that telltale tic meant. He'd had no idea what to say to her.

Though they had left the ranch house hours ago, she could still recall the way his eyes had darkened when she told him she was deaf. From shock, probably. Surprise, for sure.

She was used to both, and worse. Over the years, she'd had to explain to hundreds of people that she couldn't hear. She had built up a thick skin, an armor that protected her against any reaction.

But today, for the first time in her life, she hadn't felt ready to hear a response. And she didn't want to think about what that meant.

Nate patted her arm. "Lianne, did you tell Ryan all about the school?"

"Yes, I did." She'd better not miss a word of this conversation now. Not in front of the man sitting across from her.

Nate looked up at Ryan. "You're gonna help Daddy with the wranglers, right?"

"Right."

"And Lianne's running the ranch."

"Is she?" he asked.

"Yep. She's helping Daddy build the school. It's gonna be a camp, too. Isn't that great? But don't worry, it won't be like a *dude* ranch or anything."

Recalling her conversation with Ryan about that, Lianne couldn't keep from looking his way. He was watching her.

His hazel eyes had changed, chameleon-like, picking up the color from his T-shirt. The green of an impending storm had given way to the brighter shade of grass after the rain. The sight sent a rush of pleasure through her.

Nate patted her arm again. She tore her gaze away from Ryan.

"There will be lots of horses at the ranch, right?"

She nodded at Nate. "Right. The boys will have plenty of chances for horseback rides."

From across the lawn, Caleb and Tess approached, each carrying a tray.

"This is how you say *horse,* Ryan." Nate rested the tip of her thumb against her temple with her index and middle fingers together and standing straight up. She tapped both fingers in the air twice the way Lianne had taught her.

He nodded.

"Try it," she insisted.

"Nate," Caleb said, "why don't you give Gram and Aunt El a hand with dessert?"

"Okay," she agreed, bounding to her feet. "So long as I get the biggest piece of pie."

"We'll give that to one of our guests," her mother said. "And later you and I will have another talk about sharing."

As Nate ran off, Caleb set his tray on the picnic table. "Coffee's ready."

"Can I pour for you?" Lianne asked.

"Thanks, but I've got it covered," Caleb said. "Tess is training me."

"Yes, and it's a slow process." Tess smiled at Caleb to take the sting from her words.

Lianne smiled, too. Like Kayla and Sam, these two were lucky to have each other.

Tess turned toward Lianne. "I hope you found things okay over at the house."

"Everything's great." She spoke firmly, trying to convince herself as much as Tess. "So far I've seen everything I could possibly want in the house."

And one person she didn't want there at all.

She tried not to look at the man across the table as she reached for the mug Caleb held out to her.

She owed Caleb so much. The job. The chance to prove herself. Even the house she was living in rent-free. The big ranch house, with lots of rooms to get lost in.

Growing up with so many other kids around, she'd never had the luxury of a room to herself. Unlike Nate, she'd also never had a problem with sharing.

Before now.

Chapter Five

Their second helpings of pie finished, Ryan and Caleb had moved to a couple of lawn chairs. The one Ryan had taken provided him with a clear view of the far side of the yard, where Lianne sat at a table near a row of pine trees laced with tiny white lights. After dessert Nate had ferried Lianne over there for a sign language lesson.

Caleb's mother-in-law hefted the coffeepot. "I'll be right out with a refill."

Caleb and Tess made vague comments about continuing his "training" and followed her.

"What did you think of the dessert?" asked the older woman seated near him.

Grateful for the distraction, he turned to Tess's aunt. With her grizzled gray hair and tanned skin, Ellamae could have passed for Tony's female twin.

All during the meal, she and Roselynn had sent platters and plates and bowls of food in his direction, urging him to take extra. Three rounds later he'd finally quit saying yes. He recalled Caleb's warning that she liked to "spice things up." But after kindness like that, he was willing to give the woman the benefit of the doubt.

"Dessert was great," he said truthfully. "One of the best pecan pies I've ever tasted."

He took a long, bracing swallow of coffee. One advantage to not sleeping—no worries about too much caffeine.

Ellamae did the same, eyeing him over the rim of her mug. "You're a long way from Montana. It's your first visit to New Mexico, isn't it? And of course, your first time here in town."

"Yes, ma'am, it is." *And probably the last.* As things stood now, he knew once he'd gotten free of his obligations here, he'd never want to see the place again. Whether he went back home or not… He'd have to see how things stood then.

"You'll have to make sure and look me up next time you're in town," she said. "I'll show you around, introduce you to a few folks. And there's always something going on at the community center."

That was the last thing he needed. "Thanks. I imagine I'll be sticking close to the ranch for a while. It's a busy time over there."

Across the yard, Nate gave a loud frustrated groan.

Lianne laughed and brushed her blond hair back over one shoulder. Caleb had lit the hurricane lamps on the picnic tables, and in their glow her hair rippled like a river catching the first rays of the sun.

Fine poetic thoughts from a man whose literary heights ran to Louis L'Amour novels. And not thoughts he wanted to have at all.

"Good to know you're enjoying your new surroundings."

He'd forgotten about the woman sitting right next to him, who had trained her sharp-eyed gaze on him again. "Flagman's Folly does seem like a nice place," he said, choosing to misunderstand her. "At least, from what I've seen so far."

"Uh-huh." The ghost of a grin on her wrinkled face told him she hadn't fallen for his redirection. But she rolled with it anyway. "From what I heard around the office the other day, you got a fairly good glimpse of Signal Street."

Frowning, he looked over to Lianne and back again.

"Nope," the older woman said.

"Caleb?" Even as she shook her head, he strung her words together and made the connection. "You work at Town Hall."

She nodded. "As town clerk for more than forty years now. That's a lot of water under the bridge."

And a long history of loyalty to Judge Baylor, he'd bet. Should have heeded Caleb's warning after all.

After tonight he'd make sure to keep away from her.

"The judge has almost as much experience reading folks as I have," she said, "though he's not quite as generous in giving them the benefit of the doubt. Early on, anyway. He's seen too many situations where folks have let circumstances steer them in the wrong direction." She couldn't have made it any more clear that she knew all about his situation. And she didn't bother to hide the gleam in her eyes.

Damn him—though he wanted not to care, his desire to learn more equaled hers. "Does everybody in Flagman's Folly know what's brought me here?"

Again she shook her head. "Most folks know *Caleb* brought you here, and that's the extent of it. But he and the judge get along."

He grimaced. "Should I expect the sheriff on my doorstep at dawn?" Better that than the rude awakening the other morning.

She laughed. "Not likely. Don't take it too hard, Ryan." The kindness in her tone suddenly made him wonder about that glimmer he'd seen in her eyes.

Thinking about that glimmer suddenly made him envision Lianne standing beside the truck. He blinked and focused on Ellamae again.

"The judge provides a sounding board for a lot of folks

around here," she said. "But he knows how to keep his mouth shut."

"And you?"

"I know everything that goes on in Flagman's Folly. Sooner or later."

It hadn't escaped him that she'd left the important part of his question hanging. He understood all about folks wanting to spread gossip, good and bad, throughout their small town. Especially the bad.

Half of him wanted to say the hell with it, to walk away from this town and not look back. The other half knew he already stood on the verge of losing everything. One more wrong step, and he'd risk plunging over that edge.

OVER THE RIM of her magazine, Lianne checked out the coffee table. Napkins. One coffee mug. A carafe filled to the brim. And the full pan of brownies. Nothing to show she hadn't just settled in for a Sunday-night chocolate fest on her own.

Nothing to show she was ready and waiting.

Since their dinner at the Whistlestop a week ago, Ryan had stayed true to his word. He'd done his job and left her to do hers. Unless Caleb had a reason to talk to them together, they rarely saw each other. If their paths did happen to cross, they managed to keep the conversation civil.

When Ryan was upstairs in his bedroom, just down the hall from hers, she even did her best not to make too much noise…if she remembered. Her forgetfulness about that had been a source of never-ending complaint with Mark, too.

Maybe this sharing a house would work out.

They hadn't discussed his reaction to her being deaf. Or the fact that she was deaf. In fact, except for his momentary surprise at her announcement, whether or not she could hear hadn't seemed to register on his radar at all. A unique experience for her.

She should just give thanks for his lack of response since she'd given him the news.

But most likely, judging by her latest experience with a hearing man, they needed to get the issue out in the open. The thought had led her to detour to Harley's General Store on her way home from Kayla and Sam's this afternoon.

Despite her good intentions to watch for Ryan, he seemed to appear out of nowhere.

"Oh, hi." The tightness of her throat told her she hadn't managed a casual tone at all. She tried again. "Want a brownie?"

He couldn't mask his surprise—not from someone who depended on reading expressions the way she did. Yet even with a lifetime of experience, she couldn't quite decipher the look in his eyes.

"Yeah," he said finally. "If the coffee's on offer, too, I'll go grab an extra mug."

He left the room and she rolled her eyes and told herself to get a grip. Except she already had one on the magazine she was crumpling in her fingers. Immediately, she forced her hands to relax. This was a simple snack. He wasn't a date. She could act like a rational woman.

She fanned herself with the magazine.

Yes, he had come in and showered earlier, then gone out to the bunkhouse for dinner with the cowboys. He had done that every night this week. But this was the first time he had changed into shorts no larger than a scrap of denim and a faded blue T-shirt that clung like the plastic wrap she'd covered the pan of brownies with.

On the couch beside her, the screen of her cell phone lit up. She grabbed the phone—her lifeline, she called it. Her link to *both* her worlds, hearing and deaf. And, right now, it also provided a distraction she welcomed.

As she was responding to the text, Ryan came back with the mug. He took a chair across from where she sat on the couch.

"I just had a message." She waved with the phone and reached up with her free hand to find the lamp switch. The overhead light she had turned on earlier left his face partially shadowed—and she didn't want to miss reading a word on his lips. Or miss his lips, for that matter.

Get a grip.

She shouldn't have needed to repeat the warning. Or to have told herself the first time.

"Caleb's on his way over," she said.

"I figured he'd be spending the evening with the family."

"So did I. That's where I thought he was all day. It's the first time I've heard from him."

"He was down in Tucumcari."

"Umm...where?"

He repeated the name more slowly.

She still didn't get it but knew it was somewhere she'd never heard of. She dropped the cell phone onto the couch. "He didn't tell me his plans."

He shrugged. "Ranch business."

Meaning it didn't concern her—in his opinion. "What kind of ranch business?"

"Checking into buying a stud mare."

"Oh."

He pointed to the tray of brownies. "What's the occasion?"

"No occasion. I wanted chocolate." *And something to fortify me during this talk.* "How are things going?"

"All right." He frowned. "Why?"

"Just making conversation."

He said nothing.

She tried again. "How do you like working here?"

"Caleb has a good bunch of men on the payroll."

"I've been tied up with the contractor's crew. I haven't met any of the cowboys yet." When he said nothing, she went on, "Except Tony. I like him."

"Me, too." He poured coffee and took a sip.

"What do you think of New Mexico?"

"It's nice enough, from what I've seen so far. I haven't been anywhere but the Whistlestop and here. The environment's different. The dryness takes some getting used to."

"That's for sure." She sipped from her mug. "The other day, Caleb said you came down from his ranch in Montana. Have you got family back there?"

He had reached for the brownies and now held the knife suspended over the pan.

She waited a beat. Even though she'd asked a direct question, his lack of response almost didn't surprise her. But when he didn't move the knife, she frowned. "What's the matter?"

He looked up. "I'm deciding how big a piece to cut. You having one?"

"Yes. And I'd better get it before you and Caleb start in. I saw how much you both ate at dinner last week."

"Not our fault. Ellamae and Roselynn kept pushing seconds."

"And thirds." She took a napkin and a brownie.

He did the same and sat back in his chair. "You're from the city, you said. Chicago."

"That's right."

"The school will have lots of horses, according to Nate. You know about tending horses?"

"No, not a lot."

"Surprising, since you're running this ranch. Also according to Nate."

"Of course I'm not. I'm project manager for the school. I do office and admin work. You know that. We discussed it last week. As I recall, we discussed my qualifications then, too."

Again he said nothing. Now she could clearly see doubt in his eyes. She set her mug on the table. Hot coffee splashed onto her thumb. Nothing she couldn't handle—one wipe, one tight fist, and the crumpled napkin dropped into her lap.

"Trust me, Ryan, this project won't be a problem for me. I've worked at all kinds of jobs in my life. This isn't any harder than any of them." She forced a smile. "I waitressed in college. That's a lot tougher than maintaining a few spreadsheets."

"How did you wait tables when you couldn't hear the customers?"

Finally.

As out in the open as it could get.

He might have tried for simple curiosity in his tone. But she didn't read tones. She read body language, expressions, gazes. Now she saw stiff shoulders, a tight jaw, narrowed eyes. Resistance. And plenty of doubt.

"I'm doing fine talking to you, aren't I?" Well, fine except for the one miss—that she knew of. That happened with relying on lipreading alone.

He shrugged.

She sighed. "Look at it this way. How do you know to close the windows when there's a storm coming? Or to figure out if a horse is sick? Or to be suspicious of a shady salesman?" No sense waiting for answers she knew wouldn't come. "You use your eyes, your experience, your gut. You use whatever it takes in the situation. Right?"

Though he nodded, the slight tilt of his head said he still mistrusted her as much as he would any dishonest salesman.

She took a deep breath and let it out again. "I'm no different from anyone else. That's what I do, too. With my customers, I used what I knew, starting with reading their lips."

"Last week at the Whistlestop, I saw you struggling. Missing parts of the conversation. Not understanding everything folks said."

What he said was true—and she would never deny a natural part of her life, a part she accepted every day. But his words stung because he felt it necessary to say them. To show he thought she was less than equal.

Blinding headlights swept a path outside the house. Caleb.

She stood, looking down at Ryan. "Not everyone's easy to lip-read. In the case of my customers, I would ask them to write notes. Or have them point to what they wanted on the menu. We got the job done, just as I'll do here."

As she always did, she would show her competence through her actions. She would *prove* to this irritating cowboy that she could handle whatever came her way.

ONCE CALEB SETTLED in with his own mug and brownie, he said, "I'm leaving town in the morning, and I wanted to run a few things by you both."

"You and I already discussed our agenda for tomorrow," she reminded him. She could work just as well without him. "There's nothing on it I can't handle on my own."

"True. But I'll be gone longer than just tomorrow." He shifted in his chair so he could see them both. "I'm going to Montana again. Tess and Nate are staying since Nate still has a few weeks of school. But I'm shorthanded up north, and I can't let things slide."

"No, you can't." And with him gone, she could stay away from Ryan altogether.

"I'm headed up there tomorrow morning." He reached to pick up the leather satchel he used for his laptop.

She took a sip of coffee.

Ryan sat leaning forward, elbows on his knees and both hands wrapped around his mug, muscle ticking in his jaw. With his head tilted down, she couldn't see his eyes. Everything else screamed tension.

Caleb was watching her, waiting to continue. She flushed. How long had she been lost in thought? Had he seen her looking at Ryan?

"I know you're on top of everything we've got going regarding the school." He pulled a file folder out of his satchel and handed it across the coffee table to her. "I've looked over all the résumés and agree with your assessments."

"Great."

"And here's something new to you both." He pulled out another file. "We've got a group of scouts coming in for a week in June. All the cabins and outbuildings should be ready by then."

She nodded. "And the insurance is already in place."

"Right. It'll be a good test run." He hefted the folder. "This is contact info and the notes I made during the call."

Before she could raise her hand, Ryan reached for the file.

"Seeing as they're dudes, Tony and the boys and I will take care of this."

"I'll need the contact info," she said. "And a supply list."

"Sounds good."

Their gazes met. She dragged hers away to focus on Caleb again.

He turned to Ryan. "There's a clearly marked public trail just past the western boundary, less than a stone's throw from the supply shed we rode out to the other day. Tess and I haven't hiked it in years."

Ryan nodded. "I remember the shed. I'll check out the trail."

"Good. And while I'm gone, you're in charge here."

What did that mean? She set her mug on the table and concentrated on reading Caleb's lips.

He turned to her. "Lianne, you'll fill Ryan in on the admin part of the project, take him around the construction site, introduce him to the contractor's crew out there."

"Sure," she said, fighting to keep her expression neutral. Seeing her control over her job slip away.

"Ryan will oversee the school project, take care of anything you need. You can always reach me by email or text, but—" he looked at them both again "—unless something major comes up, I figure between the two of you, you'll be able to sort things out."

"No problem," Ryan said.

"Of course," she agreed. What else could she do?

Caleb had confirmed her fears. But as both men left the house to talk to the cowboys in the bunkhouse, irritation at Ryan overtook her.

He knew where Caleb had been today.

Had he also known this was going to happen? When he'd asked about her experience, had he been leading up to telling her the news?

Had he already wanted to show her he would be her boss?

She took a deep breath. No need to jump to conclusions, as he liked to claim she did. No need to dwell on what might have been. More than likely, he wouldn't answer her questions anyway. And she had enough to worry about going forward.

Irritation gave way to a confusing blend of anger and worry.

All this week, Ryan hadn't made an issue about her being deaf. Until tonight. How would that affect her job now that he *was* her boss?

Was he going to be just another hearing man who thought she couldn't survive in his world?

Chapter Six

Ryan stood beside the desk in the office and looked into his mug at coffee as black as his thoughts.

If not for him, Caleb wouldn't have had to leave his new family alone again. If not for the accident, *he* would still be in Montana with his family.

The boss had headed out early this morning, trusting him to take care of business. With luck, he'd fare better than he had so far. And from now on he aimed to make his own luck.

A few feet away Lianne slammed file drawers closed, one after the other.

"Is that necessary?" he demanded.

She didn't turn around, didn't pause, didn't even flinch.

Well, yeah. She couldn't hear him.

She couldn't hear the drawers slamming, either.

Or maybe that was a not-so-subtle way of making her opinion known. As unhappy as she'd been at first over their living arrangements, she couldn't feel at all pleased with the new work situation.

For a moment, he missed the smiling woman with the sparkling blue eyes and the pan of brownies. He pushed the image aside, not needing or wanting thoughts like that. Especially not since this chance Caleb had given him.

She turned from the file cabinets and moved over to the desk. "Are we finished with all this?"

"Yes. For now."

She scooped another armload of folders from the desk and began returning the files to the floor. Experience told him not to offer a hand.

Organized chaos or not, he had to admit, she knew her stuff. They had gone over detailed schedules and building plans and budgets and forecasts. She had reviewed financial spreadsheets for things he'd never heard of.

Pushing paper was only part of her job, though.

Would Caleb being away keep her from getting that job done?

He thought of the trouble he sometimes had understanding her voice. Of the times she had asked him or Caleb to repeat something. Of what she had said about waiting tables.

Would she write notes with the contractor's men if they had problems communicating? How would she handle hiring staff? Hell, how would she manage to do the thousand things needed to get the project up and running? And if she messed up...

No need to ask whose neck would land on the chopping block.

"I haven't heard from the contractor yet today." All business, she had moved on to the next item on their agenda. "He usually texts to let me know when he's coming out this way. When he plans to stop by again, I'll let you know and introduce you."

"I'll want to talk to his crew."

"Fine."

"And I'll take that file of résumés."

"The résumés?" She eyed him. "Are you sure you need to get involved with those? Caleb could be back in a week."

"Like the man said, it's springtime on a working ranch." He shook his head. "You don't know a whole lot about ranching, do you?"

Her eyes narrowed. "Is that what you were getting at last night when you asked what I knew about horses? Were you trying to put me in my place?"

So that was what had her slamming drawers this morning.

"Did you already know Caleb's plans?" she demanded.

"Hell, no."

"Well, if there's something I haven't encountered yet, I'll learn as I go. I'm a quick study."

He laughed shortly. "Are you?"

"Yes, I am. And I may not know much about horses, but I can sure recognize a horse's a—" She snapped her jaw closed. Her chest rose and fell with her deep breath.

He set his mug down and leaned over the desk. "Cussing out the boss won't look so good in your personnel file, darlin'."

"And I don't see you winning supervisor of the month." Draw.

Still, she stood there, head-to-head with him. He wasn't backing down from those pretty blue eyes.

Finally, she gave a small shrug he chose to read as an apology.

He acknowledged it with a stiff nod and picked up his mug. "Time for a break. Let's meet up tomorrow afternoon. I want a firsthand look at this project." He walked away, fighting to keep his stride easy.

Damn. He deserved everything she'd shot at him for sounding like such an ass.

He just wished her heated reply hadn't struck so close to home.

THE WALK TO the construction site took less time than it usually did, thanks to Ryan's long-legged stride. Lianne didn't ask him to slow down.

When she stopped beneath the stand of pine trees sheltering the new cabins, he continued to the expanse of open land half-cleared of brush beyond. He probably wanted to ignore her existence.

The best solution for them both.

Things had started off on the wrong foot between them from day one, and they had only gotten worse since then. Despite her caution to herself, she had let her irritation with him make her blow up in his face. He *had* acted like a horse's rear end, confirmed by the way he'd finally nodded and backed off. Still, though he'd provoked her, she couldn't stop the brief feeling of regret for what had happened.

And now this.

She could handle it. Caleb would be home…eventually. Meanwhile, she would go about her business. Do her job. And just make sure she didn't, in Caleb's words, "need anything" from the annoying man a few hundred yards away. He still stood facing away from her, looking better than any man should from this angle.

As much as she wished otherwise, she couldn't keep from enjoying the view.

He returned, gesturing over his shoulder. "What's with the clearing?"

"Caleb wants a separate corral for the school. Most of the boys will more than likely never have been on a horse. As I'd told you, we'll include lessons as part of the noncredit classes, and we plan to give them out here."

"I didn't see a corral on any of the plans."

"The contractor's not building it. The cowboys are going to take care of the job."

"Something you forgot to cover."

She shook her head. "Something I planned to tell you now."

He waved toward the cabins. "Let's have the grand tour."

"We'll start here." She pointed to one of several smaller buildings. "Everything is in different stages of completion. This is one of the student cabins. As I showed you in the plans, they're all built the same. They'll hold eight, and ten if necessary."

She went quickly through the one-room structure and then brought him to the first of the two larger buildings. "This is for the live-in staff and any local employees who might need to stay overnight on occasion."

Inside, she showed him through the large great room and the bunkrooms. They finished up in the long, narrower space that ran the length of the back of the building. "Kitchen, laundry and bathroom facilities."

He leaned against the open archway. "The dudes aren't roughing it in outhouses?"

She shook her head. "Nate and Ellamae fought for that. Tess and Roselynn were against it."

"So Caleb was the tiebreaker and wimped out."

"No, he gave me the deciding vote."

How quickly things change.

Now he'd given someone else a say over what she did. And somehow she had to get along with this man. "Since the buildings will be in use year-round, I considered indoor plumbing the logical choice." She forced a smile. "But Nate was happy to hear we'll have an outdoor shower room for the warmer weather."

"Are all the buildings this far along?"

"Not quite. It's only a small crew. But they're making good time."

"Yeah. Sounds like they're keeping busy." He gestured in the direction of the largest building. "I can hear them over there."

And she couldn't. Was that his point? "Nice to know

they don't wait till I'm walking through the door," she said evenly.

She led him out to the small porch again and turned back.

Ryan braked to a stop within inches of her. She avoided his eyes but couldn't keep her glance from sweeping his face.

Years of reading lips and expressions had left her with no doubts about what she liked best when she looked at a man. And to her dismay, Ryan Molloy fulfilled every item on her wish list. Firm, wide mouth. Strong jaw. Chin with a tiny cleft in it. Tanned skin the perfect contrast to his five o'clock shadow. His changeable eyes only made her add a brand-new item to the list.

Those eyes, stormy-green again today, stared right at her below dark brows raised in question.

Oh, please. He hadn't said anything while she was staring, had he? She couldn't have missed seeing those lips move.

She took a half step back. "I'm sorry—"

He shook his head. "No, my mistake." His rueful one-sided smile put a deep groove into his cheek. "I said something on the way out. Forgot I should have waited since you wouldn't hear me."

She wanted to shake her head, too—in confusion. At times, it didn't seem to matter to Ryan that she was deaf. But it was the other times she needed to watch out for. "What was it you'd said?"

"Why are you so caught up in this project?"

Blindsided again. She leaned back against the porch rail, hoping her surprise hadn't shown on her face. He had learned more about her than she had expected in such a short time. The thought should have unsettled her, should have warned her away.

Sunday night she had seen his doubts—in his eyes, his

posture, on his lips—even before Caleb had arrived and changed their working arrangements. Now the wrinkling of his brow said he'd asked out of pure bafflement. And maybe a genuine desire to know.

Neither of them shifted an inch, yet she would swear they had moved closer.

"It's a worthy goal," he continued. "I don't deny that. But it's a real jump for a businesswoman from Chicago. What is it that makes you care so much about overseeing this project?"

Buying some time, she boosted herself up to sit on the porch rail. She should take his interest as a positive sign. As a way to make him understand how much the school meant to her. Not the fact that it gave her the chance to prove herself. She could never tell him that. But she could let him know just enough so he would trust her to do her job. So he would back off and let her manage the project.

"Caleb's committed to the idea of this school," she began. "And so am I."

"Why wouldn't you be? It sounds like a solid investment."

"It's not just for the profits," she protested. "It's a way to change the lives of the boys who are going to stay here."

"Do you think they'll see it that way?" He settled against the railing on the opposite side of the steps and crossed his arms. "From what you've said, the kids will come here from all over the country. Won't it be tough for them to leave their homes and everyone they know?"

"That's just it. Most of them will be leaving situations they need to get away from. Neglect. Abandonment. Abuse."

"What about other issues? Won't you have to deal with things like drug and alcohol problems and criminal behavior?"

"Yes, and we're prepared to handle it. That's what we're

here for—to give them what they don't have. A safe home. Support. Adults they can trust and friends they can relate to."

He frowned. "Why do I get the feeling this is a personal issue for you?"

She hesitated and then shrugged. "It *is* personal in a way." She gestured at the row of buildings. "I know what it's like to live in an environment like this. I grew up in a residential school."

If the statement surprised him, she couldn't read it. He'd hidden his reaction as well as she'd hoped she had masked her surprise at his first question.

"Everything you plan to give the boys—is that what you needed from your school?"

She tightened her hold on the railing. Somehow he had zeroed in on one of the topics she least liked to discuss. "Yes," she said slowly, "my school provided all those things. In the beginning."

That was all she would tell him. She couldn't let him get that close.

Wishing she had kept her mouth shut and her guard up, she pushed herself off the railing before the next questions could come. As they always did. Questions she didn't want to answer for this man.

Not if he would respond the way so many others did, making it clear he saw her as different and strange. As less than whole.

Damn good save, Molloy.

He'd been so wrapped up in looking at Lianne's long blond hair fluttering as she walked that he'd gotten too close. When she abruptly stopped and turned back to him, he'd nearly run her down. Off-balance in more ways than one, when she'd asked what he had said to her, he blurted out what he'd really wanted to know. He had managed to tone his question down for her.

Why the hell did she keep fighting him?

That wouldn't get her anywhere. He was her boss now, and instead of challenging him at every turn, she ought to consider proving herself to him…just the way he was having to do—all over again—with Caleb.

As they walked toward the final structure, two-storied and larger than all the rest, she seemed determined to keep her focus on their tour. "This is the main building. The first floor is the combination mess hall and recreation center. Upstairs are the classrooms, office space and a nurse's station."

A few woodworker's tools littered either side of the school building's porch, and a sawhorse partially blocked the entrance.

She reached for it, but he stepped forward, lifted it out of the way and set it aside.

She frowned.

"I can manage something as simple as that, Ryan."

There she went again, both fists down in front of her, the way she'd done on Signal Street that first morning. "I never said you couldn't."

"Sometimes actions speak louder than words."

"Not in this case."

She eyed him for a long moment before stepping through the unfinished doorway.

He followed her into a room large enough to hold a barn dance. In one corner an open stairwell rose to the second level.

As they started toward the back of the room, a boy in his late teens appeared at the top of the stairs. He wore work boots, denim cutoffs and a carpenter's belt. "Hey, Lianne," he called. "We're up here."

Ryan tapped her shoulder. When she turned to look back at him, he pointed toward the stairs.

Changing direction, she smiled up at the kid. "Hi, Joe."

He waved at her and said, "Hey, man, if you are who I think you are, we heard about you. From Tony."

Damn. Already? The old man spent too much time running off at the mouth. "Is that so?"

"Yeah. He told us Caleb had a new foreman."

"That's right," he confirmed, making a mental apology to Tony. "Ryan Molloy."

Lianne had reached the landing. "What did you say, Joe?"

"Huh?" For a moment, he looked puzzled. "Oh, I said Caleb has a *new foreman.*" He repeated the two final words in a louder tone.

Lianne nodded.

"You know, *manager. Supervisor. Boss.*"

"I think she got it the first time," Ryan said. "And there's no need to yell."

"Whatever." He shrugged.

Lianne turned her head from the kid to him and back again. "This is Ryan."

"Yeah." The kid grinned at him.

Ryan followed Lianne's glance down a long hallway as littered as the porch had been.

"Looks like you're busy up here," she said. "I'll show him the offices another time."

He trailed her down the stairs and out to the porch again. "It also looks like they've got a way to go on these buildings."

"We'll get there," she said flatly.

"In time for the scouts?"

"Of course."

Frowning, he looked back into the building. "Mind telling me why we're changing the agenda? We could work around the mess upstairs."

She settled onto the sawhorse he had shifted and stared up at him. "Would you mind telling me what that was about with Joe?"

"What?"

"'There's no need to yell.'"

"He was getting carried away, repeating himself and raising his voice because you couldn't hear what he said."

"I didn't *see* what he said. I was watching my step climbing the stairs. He didn't realize I had my head down."

Just as he hadn't realized in the other building, speaking when she'd had her back to him. "That must happen a lot."

She shrugged. "It happens, yes. But he wasn't getting carried away. Since he thought I just didn't understand him, he was trying to help me. People do that—raise their voices with a deaf or hard-of-hearing person, thinking it will make a difference. Sometimes it does. Hearing loss covers a wide spectrum, and some deaf people can pick up a range of voices."

"Can you?"

She pressed her lips into a firm line. For a moment, he thought she wouldn't answer. Finally, she said, "No. I can't hear anyone clearly."

She'd kept her voice so low he barely caught the blurred words. Her cheeks flushed pink and her eyes glittered. Not meeting his gaze, she stood and went down the steps.

He followed, frowning again. Even with all those signals, he couldn't tell what had just happened.

Had she spoken so softly out of embarrassment because there was something she *couldn't* do?

Or to hide her anger because she'd had to admit it?

WITH BREAKFAST OVER and the day's assignments distributed among the men, Ryan got up from the table in the bunk-house kitchen and followed Tony through the door. The old man had taken a while to cross the room. He'd hung back, not wanting to rush him.

Outside, dawn had broken, and the sun had started to climb.

"You came in a little early this morning, huh?" Tony asked. "I saw you'd already had the coffee on."

"Yeah." As he had told Lianne he would do, he slept in the main house but took all his meals outside with the men… except for the night she had offered him brownies for dessert. What were the chances she'd do that again?

After the conversation on the steps of the school building yesterday, their walk back to the ranch house had gone amicably enough. He still didn't know how she felt about his question, but she seemed to have forgiven him for acting like a horse's back end.

Since then, he hadn't been able to get her out of his thoughts. Not a good thing. Along with his breakfast this morning, he had hoped company and conversation would take his mind off her.

"I took a spin to see the school yesterday," Tony said.

He smiled wryly. "Yeah, I think someone over there mentioned your name."

"Things are looking pretty good. An interesting place this ranch is gonna be with all those boys coming to stay."

He didn't care to think about the boys. Or any kids at all.

"You starting work on the corral today?"

He shook his head. "No, we've got a list of other things to do first." Things that would keep him well away from the ranch house and the construction site.

"Gotta go get that bag of new cloths I left in the truck," Tony said. "Forgot it once already."

Ryan walked alongside him, slowing down some to accommodate the other man. Tony had claimed a space for his pickup truck on the grass close to the bunkhouse, saying he liked keeping an eye on his pride and joy. Ryan suspected the proximity to the bunkhouse saved the old man's leg from extra wear and tear. And maybe, like Lianne, he didn't like to admit to some things.

As they turned back, something rustled in the underbrush alongside the bunkhouse.

"Speedy critters," Tony said, pointing at the jackrabbit now bounding across the yard.

Lianne wouldn't have heard the dry crackle of brush. All around, birds stretched their wings, mama birds chirping wake-up calls and their babies greeting the dawn, warbling songs she could never enjoy. How did she feel about missing all the sounds most people took for granted?

"You heading over to the barn?" Tony asked.

"Yeah. You?"

"I'll be along shortly. Just need one more cup of coffee to wake me up properly."

"Not me." First time in a long time he'd almost slept the night through. Only one nightmare. And he'd woken to a quiet house.

He couldn't help but smile. Now he knew why Lianne made more noise than anyone he'd ever met. She couldn't hear the racket she made.

As he left Tony at the bunkhouse, he acknowledged the plan to get her out of his thoughts had failed dismally.

As he rounded the barn, he saw his timing had only made things worse.

He froze, staring at the vision near the back porch steps.

She wore body-hugging exercise gear so shiny it seemed as though she'd oiled the blue fabric. The slanting rays of the rising sun glanced off every inch of her, making her sparkle.

When she began twisting from side to side, loosening her oblique muscles, he stepped back a pace into the shadows beside the barn, not wanting to startle her.

Okay, hell—not wanting to scare her off completely.

She went through a handful of stretches, reaching down to set her palms almost flat on the ground to elongate her spine, stretching up to the sky, unknowingly offering him full view of every sun-sparkled curve of her silhouette. Her limbs moved as easily as a puppet's dangling from its strings, while every last muscle in him tightened in response.

A quick jog took her to the top of the porch steps. She lowered herself into a crouch and then sprang up to grab the edge of the porch roof and heave her body into chin-up position.

His mouth opened in stunned surprise until he found the wits to close it again. His feet might have put down roots. Nothing short of an earthquake would get him to shift from that vantage spot.

No need to spare a moment for guilt. Any cowhands arriving at the barn the way he had would see her. Any driver or rider coming far enough up the driveway would have the back porch in full view. Still, he couldn't deny the sudden fierce hope that this was a sight meant just for him.

Her exercises had started his blood pumping, too. Soon they had his breath trapped in his chest.

She worked through a series of yoga stretches, her gestures unhurried and graceful, as if she moved to music only she could hear. Eyes closed, she kept her face toward the sun, letting its rays wash over her. The gleam of reflected light dazzled him.

He clenched his fists, wishing he could take the place of the sun and touch everywhere that light fell, wanting to run his fingers down her lean limbs and to warm her soft, cool curves with his hands.

Sweat broke out on his forehead.

Overseeing the project manager had damn sure taken on new meaning.

He stepped farther back into the shadows, slumped against the side of the barn and dragged his shirtsleeve across his brow.

Chapter Seven

Later that afternoon Ryan stood in the office doorway and looked in surprise at the bare desk. A big change from the flood of files she normally kept all over its surface. Not to mention the floor.

Better to think of that mess than to dwell on the vision he'd seen after breakfast.

Hell, he'd seen a lot more of a lot of women than he'd seen of Lianne. But somehow that glimpse of her in her exercise gear had darned near knocked his legs out from under him.

The view now had him a little shaky, too.

Behind the desk, she stood studying a spreadsheet, her blond hair pushed back to spill around her shoulders. With her head tilted down, one long strand had slipped forward near her temple and draped down against her cheek. Idly, she twirled the strand around and around a pencil.

Eventually she looked up and noticed him leaning against the doorjamb. Blue eyes observed him without blinking. Pink lips stayed straight and firm. But he could see she was making an effort.

He gestured around the room. "What happened to organized chaos?"

"Sometimes I like a rest from it."

"I'll bet."

She laughed.

The soft, blurred sound had his legs even shakier. "How's it going?"

"About the same as it was this morning. And again right after lunch." She pointed toward her computer monitor at the digits in the corner of the screen. "Two hours ago, that is."

"That long already?"

"Not nearly long enough."

She tossed her pencil onto the desk. The lead broke. Sighing, she shook her head. "Good thing there are plenty more where that one came from. Which reminds me, Ryan. Do you think with the next supply order, I should purchase a time clock? Maybe if I punch in and out, you won't need to check up to see when I'm working."

Was that the beginning of a curve to those pink lips?

"Very funny." He shifted the spreadsheet and sat on one edge of the desk. "Not checking up, supervising," he corrected. "And I'll take that stack of résumés from you."

The curve shifted back to a straight line, but she went to the file cabinet by the credenza for a folder and set it on the desk. "Those are mostly candidates for the aides—the counselor positions for the noncurricular activities. Caleb has reviewed them. I'm starting with the top few."

"How are you planning to contact the applicants?"

"I've already called the first two."

"'Called?'" Frowning, he looked at the telephone she had pushed to one corner of the desk and half buried under a sheaf of papers. "On the phone?"

"No. Through video relay." She pointed toward the computer again. "I sign to an online interpreter who speaks for me and tells me what the other party says. The conversation goes back and forth, just as in any phone call."

He nodded. The explanation sounded like something

she'd memorized, but it did address one of the issues he'd wondered about—how she would deal with hiring the staff. "You'll do the interviews through the interpreter."

"No. Those I'll handle face-to-face. I've confirmed a couple for next week."

He nodded. "I'm planning some full days out on the ranch, but I'll work around your schedule. Give me the dates."

"Why? I'm not expecting you to sit in on the interviews."

"That's what supervisors do."

She shook her head emphatically, sending that strand of hair swinging against her cheek. "Not in this case. I've already talked to Caleb about the candidates. He's good with my selections." She shoved a file drawer closed. Metal clanged.

At the desk again she slipped her spreadsheet into a folder, as if worried he'd manhandle the paperwork from her. As if afraid he'd try to take over her job.

He had a job to do, too, dammit.

While I'm gone, you're in charge here.

The boss might as well have said "I'm putting you to the test."

Again.

"We've had this conversation before, Lianne. Caleb left me to oversee the project."

"Yes, I know." She sighed. "It's an entry-level staff position. I can do the interviewing on my own."

No fists this time, but he could see them in his mind. "Regardless, I'll be here. Besides, you might want an independent observer in the room." He tried a smile again. "When you're talking to someone you may decide to hire, you want to make sure you stay professional."

She laughed. "We've had that conversation before, too.

Don't you remember? I *am* a professional. And I know how to act while I'm interviewing."

"Think so? Well, here's a tip you might find helpful. Keep your hands away from your face. Especially when you're holding a pencil."

Her eyes narrowed then widened in sudden understanding. She rubbed her cheek with her fingertips.

"Missed it." He reached up and lightly brushed aside her tendril of hair, then thumbed away the dark smudge on her temple.

Her eyes met his. Her pink lips softened, and his pulse gave one mighty hitch.

She stepped back, breaking contact, looking away. "I'd better go check in a mirror." She moved past him, leaving behind the faint scent of roses.

And one thoroughly shaken man.

LIANNE FOUND HER bag in the kitchen where she had left it. She quickly checked in her compact mirror to make sure the pencil smudge was gone and then headed out the back door.

As far as she was concerned, her conversation in the office with Ryan had ended. And whatever else had just started in there wasn't going to continue.

One hand touching her cheek, she walked into the yard, warmed by the late-afternoon sun. Blue sky and white clouds stretched overhead. In the distance a tree-covered ridge beckoned. One day, she would check it out. But for now, with any luck, she'd already gotten far enough from Ryan.

Outside the barn, Tony sat on a low stool, doing something that required a tub of soapy water.

When he saw her approaching, he smiled. "Hey there. Come to keep an old man company?"

No, to leave a younger man behind.

"You're not old, Tony. You're just mature for your age."

He laughed.

She, on the other hand, had acted immaturely—like a schoolgirl swooning because the boy she had a crush on had just smiled at her. But Ryan hadn't smiled. He'd touched.

All her years of reading faces had told her he'd wanted more. And, all right—*yes,* she'd wanted that, too.

She swung herself up onto the top rail of the corral. From here she would have the back porch of the house in view.

Tony would be good company right now. As busy as he was, he wouldn't notice her distraction. And since he couldn't look at her and work at the same time, they couldn't carry on a conversation.

But she'd forgotten how much he liked to talk.

"Went for a look over at the school the other day. They've made some progress since I was out there a while back. Things all going well with the construction, I take it?"

She nodded.

"Caleb's left the place in good hands."

She smiled and then wondered whether he'd meant hers or Ryan's. Right now she didn't want to think about Ryan or his hands. Or his eyes or his mouth or his anything else.

"Everything going well with you, too?" Tony asked.

"Yes. Why?" She frowned. She'd just sounded as suspicious as Ryan had the night she'd tried to make conversation over the brownies. "Things are fine. Any reason for asking?"

"Nope. Bet you're happy to be staying in that house over there."

Why? This time, she didn't ask, but she shot a glance in that direction. All clear, fortunately.

"I mean, it's nice for you being close by with your sister

getting ready to have her baby. You'll still be here for the occasion, won't you?"

"Oh, yes, I will," she confirmed, trying to push away a sudden rush of guilt. She and Kayla texted several times a day, but she hadn't gone to visit her since…since Caleb had made Ryan her boss. She wasn't sure if she could keep her feelings out of her voice well enough to prevent Kayla from noticing.

"It's a lot different here than up in Chicago, isn't it? I've never been that far north before. And tell you the truth, I'm just as glad to live where it stays warm for a good part of the year." He pushed himself to a standing position, one foot on the ground, the other, the boot with the raised heel, still propped up on the rung of his stool.

He smacked that leg with the soft cloth in his hand. "This one's giving me trouble right now. Can't even stand up like a proper gentleman. No way to treat a lady."

"You're always a perfect gentleman with me."

Smiling, he tipped his cowboy hat to her and then started toward the barn.

Sometimes when they talked, he would mention his leg. Sometimes he wouldn't. That was his choice, just as choosing how much to say about her abilities was her decision.

Out by the school, when Ryan had asked whether or not she could hear a person's voice, she had chosen to answer. In fact, she'd responded to all of his questions, even the ones that had thrown her off-balance—which meant most of them. He had the knack of asking things no one else had ever thought to, or of asking them in a different way than anyone had before.

He had the knack of making her think things she shouldn't.

Right now, as she looked up and saw him crossing the

yard toward her, he made her think she should have followed Tony into the barn.

Since that really would look like running, she stood her ground.

"Thought you were coming back to the office."

"I thought we were done."

He stopped in front of her, light from the lowering sun on his face but his Stetson putting his eyes in shadow. She could read his lips but missed the stormy-green of his eyes.

"Yeah, we were done." Considering the set of his jaw, he had spoken grimly. "Lianne...about what happened—"

"Nothing happened," she said quickly, "except that we both learned something new. I learned to keep a pencil out of my hand when I'm conducting an interview."

His line. His turn now.

I learned to keep my hands off you.

But his lips didn't move.

AFTER A MORNING spent with half his small crew in the far northern acres, Ryan headed back to the main house, letting the stallion take him home. He took a swig from the water bottle he'd learned to carry at all times to combat the dryness of the Southwest. No breeze moved the cotton-ball clouds. No air moved at all except for a shimmery haze generated by the heat of the sun.

It was only early May. What would things be like here in the dog days of summer?

A horse and rider came into view from the west, riding hard.

He swallowed against a sudden rush from the past....

Standing on the north ridge, where cell phone reception didn't exist, spotting the horse and rider that would bring him the message no one ever wanted to hear. Making his own breakneck rush to the ranch and the pickup truck and the road into town. And finally, reaching the claustrophobic waiting room where a sad-eyed surgeon fought exhaustion and watched him fight back tears.

He blinked, sharpening his gaze.

This rider wasn't headed his way. Judging by the angle, they would cross paths close to the ranch house. One of the hands, most likely, though he couldn't tell from this far away. He'd given both crews his location today. They'd know where to find him in an emergency. But the rider hadn't come from that direction.

He kept the stallion at a steady canter.

The other horse gained ground. Now he could see the rider more clearly, a slim figure with flowing hair.

Lianne.

A few days ago she had shied away from his touch like a frightened filly. He hadn't misread her first reaction, though. The look on her face as she had fled the room only confirmed what her eyes had revealed. Interest. Attraction. And dismay.

He'd had no trouble recognizing those feelings in her expression; he'd been hit with a healthy shot of all three himself.

The days spent working in the north pastures had put some distance between them but not nearly enough. He wasn't sure any amount of distance could take him far enough away.

He'd managed to keep himself from hanging around the barn, in view of the back porch, at daybreak. And now whenever they met in the office, he made damn sure to keep his hands to himself.

What was she doing out here?

The stallion overtook her horse with ease. Both animals pranced, ready for a competitive run. He reined in until they settled alongside each other, head to tail, leaving him facing Lianne.

Her cheeks looked rosy, either from fresh air or exercise—

He reined in this new vision as sharply as he had the stallion. "You should let me know if you plan to go off on your own."

"I'm entitled to a lunch hour."

"That's not what I meant. Suppose your horse threw you? Or went lame? There's plenty of good riding out here, but it pays to keep aware of the dangers."

She patted the cell phone clipped to the waistband of her jeans. "I never go anywhere without this."

"The damned things don't always work."

To his surprise, she simply nodded.

"Thought you didn't know how to ride." He'd managed to say the words mildly this time.

She ran her hand along her horse's mane. "I'm not sure where you got that idea. You said, 'You know about tending horses?' And I said, 'No, not a lot.' I didn't say anything about not knowing how to ride."

"Good memory." She'd replayed their statements word for word. "They have horses in Chicago?"

"I'm sure they have stables somewhere. That's not where I ride."

The stallion moved restlessly beneath him.

Ryan looked toward the pine- and piñon-covered ridge just past the western boundary. "I'm planning to check out that hiking trail Caleb mentioned. You game?"

Eyes gleaming, she nodded.

Hadn't he known she would agree? She wouldn't want to be left out of anything connected to her project.

He gestured to the west. "That way."

She took off, not looking back to make sure he followed. He watched with a critical eye to see how she handled the mare. She had nice hands and a good seat.

He spent so much time checking out her riding form, he didn't realize she'd left him in the dust—until he found himself choking on it.

Shaking his head, he followed.

Chapter Eight

As the trail narrowed, the man beside her moved to take the lead. Had she really expected anything else?

Swallowing her irritation, Lianne fell into step behind him.

When she had decided on an early lunch and asked Tony to saddle a horse for her, she hadn't planned to have company on the ride. Hadn't *wanted* company.

But despite everything she'd said to herself for days now about staying away from Ryan, the sight of him on the horizon had made her pulse race with pleasure.

Ahead of her he climbed over a tree limb that had fallen across the trail. He turned back, reaching out to her.

She shook her head. "I've got it." She easily scaled the prickly branches and landed beside him.

He started forward again. For a long moment she stood there, staring after him. *It pays to keep aware of the dangers,* he had warned. Little did he know, all the danger she faced right now came from *him.*

As she had urged her horse into a gallop toward this ridge, knowing Ryan would follow, she'd hoped he would leave his doubts about her behind.

But what were the chances of that?

She sipped from her water bottle and resumed her climb.

A few minutes later he stopped and pointed ahead of them. "The incline's getting steeper."

"Bring it on," she said, unable to hold back a grin. "If you think this little hill scares me, you can think again."

He smiled, widely enough to make his eyes crinkle at the corners, as if he liked the challenge.

When he turned away, she fanned herself and continued onward. Or upward. The incline didn't bother her, but the heat was climbing faster than they did. Or maybe Ryan's nearness had raised her temperature. No matter how much he infuriated her—and, oh, he did infuriate her—there was a lot to like about the man.

As the ground leveled out near the peak of the mountain, she quickly slipped her hands beneath her hair to adjust her hearing aids. A conversation wouldn't register, but the aids picked up other sounds.

They were at a designated lookout on the well-marked trail with a concrete picnic table and benches cemented into a solid base.

Ryan leaned against a rock outcropping near the table, close to a flowing stream.

"Oh, yes." She went down on one knee beside the stream and used both hands to splash water on her face. When she stood, she wiped the back of her arm across her forehead, scattering drops. "Hot!"

"Yeah." He looked down into the water.

Another tree limb had fallen or been dragged onto one of the benches. Avoiding the sticky pine, she moved to the other side and took a seat. To her dismay, he followed. He swung one booted foot over the bench and straddled it, looking in her direction.

She looked at the water bottle she had set on the table. Yes, her hearing aids allowed her to pick up some sounds or, more often, vibrations. But she didn't need *anything* to be aware of his nearness.

He touched her arm, probably trying to get her attention. Stray water drops scattered beneath his warm hand. Without thinking, she tilted her head just a bit, remembering that hand on her cheek.

After a moment, she turned reluctantly to look at him.

"We can't talk if you can't see me," he said.

"I could have seen you just as well from where you were standing."

"This is easier."

Not for me.

If she talked, she wouldn't have to stare at his lips, so close to hers. She brushed at the dampness on her arm. "Too bad it's not monsoon season here yet. We could use a good storm. For the humidity."

How stupid, to be talking of the weather.

Inane or not, it took her right back to that first day on Signal Street.

In the bright sunshine that morning, this cowboy's eyes had been that odd stormy-green, the color of the clouds that sometimes rolled in over Lake Michigan, carrying with them the scent of rain and the promise of an electrical storm.

"I love a good lightning storm," she said. "All those sudden crackles and brilliant spikes. I love thunderstorms even more. I can feel the vibrations in the air. Sometimes, I can hear the thunder when it booms."

And that day, standing close to this man, she had heard the thunder in his voice and felt it vibrate through her. Somehow she had known he could bring more trouble to her than a lightning strike and cause more harm than the most violent storm.

How right she had been.

She looked around them, searching for something else

to say. "This ought to be a good trail for the scouts. Not too tough. Not too dangerous."

He touched her arm. "Good for the kids from the school, too, I'd think."

She nodded and focused on her bottle.

He brought her attention back to him.

This was ridiculous. She couldn't keep talking to the space in front of her just so she could avoid looking his way. And having him touch her again and again was more dangerous than their climb.

She turned slightly on the bench. Inches separated them, yet she could feel the warmth of him against her knees. She wouldn't let that distract her from a simple conversation.

"How old were you," he asked, "when you started going to the residential school?"

Maybe not so simple.

Half of her wanted to run. The other half wanted to get closer to him. None of her had the nerve to meet his eyes again. She focused on his mouth and gave him the answer she had long ago memorized. "I lived with my family till I was six. Then I moved to the school."

He pursed his lips, maybe in a whistle, but she couldn't tell. "They just sent you away? That young?"

The concern in his face made her throat tighten. "It wasn't a bad thing. They did what they thought was best for me."

She could see him turning that over in his mind. She could see the questions forming. He would ask her about her deafness. He would want to know how she felt about not being able to hear.

"Did you live in a dorm?"

Yet another question that threw her off-balance. She nodded.

"What was that like?"

She paused to think. No one had ever asked her to describe dorm life. "It was…crazy. Comforting. Definitely lacking in privacy. And a lot of fun."

"You didn't miss your family?"

"Of course I did. At first. Especially my sister, Kayla. She's two years younger. But the longer I stayed at school and the more comfortable I felt communicating in sign, the more I wanted to be there. With people who could understand me." Those were the days before she had focused on all those speech lessons. Before she had worked so hard to learn to read lips.

"But you went home for holidays. And in the summer." His expression told her he had put these as statements, not questions, because of course he would assume she had gone to see her family on school breaks.

"At first I did," she said again. "But as I got older, I wanted to stay with my friends. It was…" She ran her finger over the torn label on her water bottle. *It was* my *choice,* she planned to say, *not my family's.*

Had she been going on too long? Babbling? Was this really such a good idea, to be sharing so much of her past with this man?

She made the mistake of looking into his eyes again.

Shrugging, she confessed, "It wasn't a popular decision. They weren't happy that I chose not to go home." She didn't want to talk about her father's arguments and her stepmother's pleas. She wouldn't think about Kayla's tears. "It was something I had to do. But when it was time to start high school, I went back to live with my family again permanently."

"That was a long time away."

"Yes."

"After all those years, what made them bring you home again?"

"They didn't. By that time, I wanted to go back. I loved my teachers and all my friends, but when I hit my teens, things changed, and I got the urge to experience something else."

For the first time, she'd wanted a life outside that school.

"Sounds like you hit a rebellious streak."

"Maybe. Though my teachers always said I knew my own mind too well. Like Nate." She laughed. "Whatever you would call it, I don't know." Her smile slid away. Because she *did* know.

Another truth. This time one she had never shared with anyone.

She took a deep breath and let it out. "I started to feel restless and boxed in there. Closed off from the rest of the world."

He swung his leg over the bench, resting his back against the edge of the table. He was facing her directly now. She couldn't avoid seeing his lips. Or his eyes.

"A lot of the other kids probably felt the way you did."

"It's possible. I'm not sure. They all stayed on until graduation." She shrugged and ran her fingers over the water bottle. "But I felt as though I didn't belong there anymore. I could read lips with more accuracy than anyone at school, including some of my teachers, and that made me…different."

"You *are* different."

Straightening her shoulders, she waited for what always came next. Again his response surprised her.

"That stands to reason, doesn't it?" He reached up and smoothed a strand of her hair. "No two people are exactly alike. No two people have your blue eyes." Lightly, he touched her temple.

Her scalp prickled.

"No two people have this nose." He brushed the tip of it with his finger.

She swallowed a nervous laugh.

"And definitely, no two people have these lips." He outlined her bottom lip with his thumb.

No laughter now. She couldn't even force a smile.

He cupped her chin with his hand.

A shiver ran through her. Pleasure? Caution? She couldn't tell.

Along with all their run-ins and arguments and their up-and-down working relationship, hadn't she been fighting her own attraction to him? When she accepted his offer to ride here, hadn't she hoped something like this would happen?

His warm fingers supported her chin, holding her mouth ready for his. When she closed her eyes, he brushed his free hand across her cheek, his thumb rough yet gentle.

Their lips met, and the kiss was warm and sweet and filled with desire. His and hers.

When she opened her eyes again, he stayed close. So close she could see every one of his long dark lashes. So close she could see the stormy-green she had known all along would bring her nothing but trouble.

Shifting on the bench, she sighed and shook her head. "We can't do this."

She rose and moved away, took another mouthful of water, hoped to wash away the delicious taste of him. Then she paced the length of the clearing beside the bench, knowing she didn't have to look his way for him to get her message. "That was nice, Ryan. Very nice. I won't deny it. But you know we can't do this. After all, we can't even get along with each other for more than two days in a row."

She was babbling again, saying too much. Which of them was she attempting to convince?

Yes, they fought. And yes, he was her boss—sometimes

too much her boss with his infuriating way of taking over. She'd be a fool to let this go anywhere.

Think about the future, about making the school a success. For Caleb. For the kids.

For me.

Giving in to this attraction to Ryan could jeopardize all that.

She stopped pacing and met his gaze. "We work together, Ryan. That—" She gestured toward him. "Nice as it was, that can't happen again. We've got too much at stake."

He nodded, his expression bleak.

Or did she only imagine that because she hoped he felt as disappointed as she did?

Turning away, she started down the trail on her own.

WHEN HE GOT up to leave the bunkhouse after lunch, Tony tagged along. It had become a regular habit of the old man's.

"Talked to Caleb lately?" Tony asked.

"Yeah, yesterday." He shut the door behind them and struggled to think. With…other things on his mind, he'd forgotten to tell the men at lunch. And breakfast. "He's coming back for a while at the end of the month."

"Sounds good."

"We're sticking to the short crew for the summer. He's holding off on buying stock, wants to focus on getting the school up and running." More reason to keep an eye on the construction. And they wouldn't lack for chores to keep them busy, including that corral.

Halfway to the barn, Tony eyed him. "You and Lianne go out riding together this morning?"

The man asked his question as casually as if, like these chats on the porch, his going riding with Lianne had become just another daily occurrence. The truth was that they hadn't been riding again since the day of the incident. And that day, although he and Lianne had returned to the ranch at the same time, they hadn't talked on the way back from the ridge. He'd had a feeling she would've liked to have left him in the dust again, too.

He swallowed a sigh. He didn't want to think about Lianne. Bad enough he'd had to face her every day since then.

Since his latest wrong move with one of Caleb's employees.

"No," he said flatly. "She probably ran into town. Or out to her sister's."

"Maybe. She hasn't been around. Since you both came riding in together that day, I figured you might've gone out again."

Not wanting to cut the old man off but not wanting to hear him running on about Lianne, either, he said, "I was working out by the corral all morning."

Just before noon he'd come in and taken a shower at the house. He hadn't seen her at all. Hadn't heard her, either.

He took a swig from the water bottle he'd carried from the bunkhouse, needing to do something with his hands. It seemed as if every time he *did* think of her, he wanted to touch her.

What a damned fool.

They'd reached the barn, and Tony stood eyeing him.

"The reason I asked about you and Lianne…"

That was Tony. Never would quit till he'd had his say. "Yeah?"

"You missed a visitor while you were gone."

"Who would that be?"

"Feisty gray-haired woman. Walked right into the barn like she owned it. Said she was Caleb's aunt."

"Sounds like her. Ellamae?"

"That would be the one."

He hadn't seen her since the night at the Whistlestop Inn.

Counting back, he frowned. A few weeks ago now, that was. He'd have expected her out here before now. Much before.

"She and I had quite a little talk," Tony said.

Between the two of them, they'd probably covered any news to be had in Flagman's Folly. Including his? But Tony wasn't acting any different than usual. "I don't know why she would've come to the barn. She must've been looking for Lianne."

"She made a point of saying she wanted to talk to you. Said she'd stop by again soon. Speaking of feisty women," Tony went on, "Lianne's got some pluck, too. Y'know, after you went off to the bunkhouse that day, I stayed working in here. A while later she marched in—just like that Ellamae— and said she wanted me to show her how to groom a horse."

"Did she?"

"Yep. And she wouldn't let me do a thing for her."

"Yeah. That sounds like her, too." He shook his head. "How did you…explain things?"

"Didn't have to. Like I said, she wanted me to show her. I took one horse, she took another. She just watched me and followed along."

I can handle this.

The near-empty water bottle crackled as he squeezed it in his fist.

He wouldn't care to swear in Judge Baylor's courtroom whether the automatic reaction came from irritation or anger. Most likely a bit of both, along with a good measure of disgust.

With himself.

What the hell kind of man was he? How could he lust after another woman when he hadn't yet come to terms with losing his wife and child?

He entered the ranch house and trudged up the stairs.

Lianne had the right idea. He had kissed her, and she had thought of her job.

That was where his head should have been, too, instead of getting wrapped up in her story. Instead of getting caught by the vulnerability in her eyes.

Halfway up the stairs, he heard the sound of water running. A few steps down the hall, he saw the bathroom door standing ajar, revealing only the steam-misted mirror and a pile of clothing perched haphazardly on the edge of the sink.

As he went to pass the door on the way to his room, Lianne moved into view, her back to him. He stopped dead in his tracks. If she could have heard his footsteps, she would already have pushed the door closed. That fact made him think twice about standing there looking.

But like a hog-tied bull, he couldn't have broken free if he'd tried.

Plump water drops trickled along her shoulders and arms. Wet hair streamed down her bare back, dampening the towel she'd wrapped low on her hips. This was worse than the morning he'd stood out in the open watching her stretch in the sun.

Hell, no. It was much better.

Water dribbled down the steam-fogged mirror, leaving tiny tracks that offered tantalizing views. His mouth went so dry he'd have willingly licked some of that moisture away if only he could have gotten into the room.

Still unaware of him, she poured lotion into her hand, then rubbed her palms together and leaned down to run both hands over her calves, leaving twin creamy white streaks behind.

He shoved his hands into his back pockets.

Without any help from him at all, the fog on the mirror began to clear.

As she bent from the waist, massaging the lotion into her

skin, the edge of the bathroom counter blocked his view of all but the curved tops of her breasts and the start of the deep V plunging between them.

He couldn't take much more of this torture. He couldn't stay there, either, without feeling like the world's biggest heel.

The last thought gave him the strength to back away.

Somehow he found the wits to get past the door and down the hall and into his room.

Chapter Nine

Ryan stood just outside the office, bracing himself.

When Lianne finally spotted him standing in the doorway, she looked him up and down, from the fresh Western shirt and jeans he'd put on after his shower to the spit-polished pair of boots that had never seen a stirrup or spur.

"What are you doing here?"

He made a show of looking at his watch. "I'm early for the interview."

"I thought we'd decided I could handle these myself."

"You decided. I'm here."

"Ryan—"

The lamp near the coffeemaker began to flash rapidly at the same time the doorbell rang. He frowned. A short in the wiring?

"It's connected to the bell," she said, as if she'd read his mind. "You must not be the only one early for the interview." She brushed past him, looking good in a button-down white silk shirt, a black skirt and low heels that still managed to make her long legs look longer.

When he realized he'd stood staring till she got all the way to the front door, he hustled into the room.

Taking the power position in the desk chair would be a nice touch. But on second thought, he decided to stand. He leaned against the credenza behind the desk and crossed his arms.

Lianne came into the room with a teenaged boy who looked as spit-shined as Ryan's boots and not yet half as old.

"Ryan, this is Billy Maxwell."

Billy.

Ryan froze, his hand half-outstretched.

A familiar name—but not one from the stack of résumés she'd given him. If it had been, he'd never have forgotten.

He shook hands with the kid and returned to his seat again.

Lianne looked at him. "Wouldn't you prefer a chair?"

"No, I'm fine."

She sat behind the desk and the kid took one of the chairs at the front.

Jaw clamped tight, he watched and listened as they chatted about folks in town and the kid's graduation, coming up later in the month.

Good way to break in the ice, get the applicant comfortable. She had the right idea. But when the chat went on and the interview questions never began, he frowned.

When they both finally stopped for breath, he said, "Did you bring a résumé with you?"

Billy looked up. "No, I didn't."

Lianne glanced over her shoulder at him. "Ryan…" She gestured to the vacant chair beside Billy's.

He waved the offer away and looked at the kid. "Where are you working now?"

"At Harley's General. On Signal Street."

"What's your position?"

Lianne rose and moved to stand beside the filing cabinet.

"It's a grocery store," Billy said. "I work the register there after school and on weekends."

He nodded. "Have you got any other experience? Have you worked with troubled teens before?"

Billy shook his head.

Lianne opened a drawer in the cabinet and pulled out a folder. She plucked a sheet of paper from it and handed it to the kid. "Billy, I appreciate your taking the time to stop by this afternoon. We're asking applicants to complete this form. You're working tomorrow, aren't you?"

He nodded.

"Great. If you'll take this with you and fill it out, I'll pick it up from you at Harley's."

The kid nodded and shook hands with Ryan. Lianne escorted him from the room.

Ryan settled back on the credenza.

She returned within two minutes, stalking in on those heels. "Ryan." She took a deep breath. "What is this?" She gestured at him, indicating his seat on the credenza and his crossed arms.

"It's comfortable."

"It's intimidating, especially for someone who doesn't have much experience with interviews."

"You told me you knew what you were doing."

"Very funny." But she didn't smile. "I sincerely hope the next interviews go better than this one did," she said. "And that you'll reconsider what it means to work together."

He'd have bristled at the words if her voice hadn't suddenly gone low and soft.

She sighed. "If you sit behind me, I can't participate in the conversation very well."

Hell. The day at the construction site all over again. She couldn't see the kid when she'd climbed the stairs. She couldn't hear what *he'd* said to her when he'd almost run her down. Just as he had then, he said, "I forgot."

"You forgot."

"Yeah."

Her eyes glistened. And just like that day at the site, he didn't get why.

She shook her head. "Whatever. I'm not sure I understand what you were trying to do. Why did you jump in with those questions?"

He shrugged. "I thought you were floundering, so I asked the questions."

"To help me?"

"To do my job."

Her eyes gleamed again. She nodded shortly and left the room.

He gripped the edge of the credenza with both hands. The woman was going to drive him to distraction. Did she honest-to-Pete think she'd catch him with that bear trap of a question?

Yeah, he'd wanted to help her.

But that would be the last thing she'd want to know.

RYAN FINISHED OUTLINING the plans for tomorrow with the rest of the cowhands, then left the bunkhouse with Tony.

The old man began rehashing the events of his day and sharing whatever info, news and just plain gossip he had collected since their last talk.

Ryan never begrudged any of the time he spent here. But tonight, as he'd done so many times lately, he wished he didn't have to fight to keep his mind from wandering.

The day of the interviews, the second one had gone worse than the first. Lianne hadn't been able to read the applicant well at all, and he'd jumped in to help—damn the consequences.

He'd been dealing with the effects of his action since last week.

Their meetings ran strictly along business lines. Clipped

discussions about the scouts and the school. Battles over whose job covered what responsibilities. Nothing personal. Nothing involving brownies and a cup of coffee. Nothing even close to a nice relaxed chat on the porch.

He shoved himself away from the railing. "I'll see you in the morning."

"You heading over to the house?"

"Don't I always?" He eyed the old man. Neither of them needed to stop by the barn at the moment, which was why, as usual, they had settled against the rails. Tony didn't jump in to respond, which wasn't usual at all.

Maybe his leg was acting up again. There wasn't much likelihood of the old man raising the subject in front of the cowhands. "You doing all right? Need some time off? I can get one of the boys to take over in the barn tomorrow."

After Tony's denial and a few more minutes on the porch, he crossed the yard and passed the barn on his way to the main house. By now his boots probably could've taken him there on autopilot.

This time, determination drove him. If he was ever going to prove to Caleb he could be trusted, he needed to get along with all the men—and the one woman—he supervised.

That meant getting control of this situation with Lianne, getting to know her—in a head-straight, hands-off way. Working with her, not butting heads on a regular basis. They needed to go somewhere besides the ranch, away from the triggers that kept them from having a normal conversation with each other. Away from the antagonism in that damned office.

Supper out would be the place to start. Neutral territory. A nice meal. Dessert… Something chocolate.

Inside the house, he found the office empty, the computer shut down and the desk completely cleared of paperwork.

He had no better luck in the kitchen.

That all changed when he returned to the living room and looked through the stair railing.

He saw her feet first, encased in strappy sandals with high heels. Then her legs, impossibly long and firm, going on until they finally disappeared beneath the edge of a green skirt that hugged her hips. A pale green top took care of snuggling the rest of her, and a waterfall of fresh-washed honey-blond hair tumbled around her shoulders.

She paused at the bottom of the stairs.

He reached up to loosen his tight collar…and found his work shirt already unsnapped. "Don't you look nice."

"Thanks."

When she passed him, her rose-scented perfume drifted over to him. He leaned back against the stair rail and crossed his arms.

She took the chair closest to the door, easing onto the seat as if afraid of wrinkling her skirt.

He made a sweeping gesture, indicating her outfit. "Have plans for the night?"

She nodded.

Right. He wasn't winning any awards for originality in this conversation. That didn't matter, as long as he got to his goal. "I'd thought we might go out for a meal." He shoved his hands into his pockets. "Maybe another time."

"Maybe that's not such a good idea." She dropped a satiny bag in her lap and smoothed her hands along her skirt.

"What's wrong with having a meal?" he asked. "We spend plenty of time together on the ranch."

"For business reasons."

"Exactly. That's just what I'm saying. We've had plenty of business meetings."

"Oh, yes. Usually several times a day." Her smile looked strained. He caught some additional tension beneath her words.

He'd felt plenty of stress lately, himself. "We haven't spent much time together other than briefings in the office or going over to the construction site."

Or hiking the trail.

She said nothing. He could sense her backing away.

"After all," he said, "we're working together. We ought to get to know each other. Go out to supper or for coffee once in a while, the way I go for a few beers with Tony and the guys."

She stared back at him silently.

He heard the sound of a car driving up to the front of the house, followed by the vibration of her cell phone.

She reached into the bag on her lap and pulled out her cell phone, read the incoming message, and smiled—*smiled, dammit*—as she tapped the keys.

He held his frustration in check. He had too much riding on this to mess it up.

Done with the phone, she dropped it into her bag. She rose from the chair and smoothed her skirt. Finally, she said, "I'll think about it."

RYAN HAD JUST finished brewing a pot of coffee when a knock came at the back door.

Lianne.

She'd changed her mind. Canceled her date. Sent the guy—whoever he was—packing. After she'd seen the kitchen light on, she had come around to the back of the house because…she'd…forgotten her key.

Yeah, right.

Still, smiling, he went to the back door and opened it.

"Glad you're so happy to see me." His visitor stood on the porch, looking up at him.

"Why wouldn't I be?" He stepped back. "But what are you doing here?"

Waving a deck of cards at him, Tony made his way across the room. "The boys are playing poker. I prefer a nice game of gin rummy."

"Since when?"

The old man sat heavily in one of the oak kitchen chairs and slapped the deck on the table. "Since I saw that car drive off."

He eyed him. "You couldn't have seen a car from the bunkhouse."

Tony shrugged and began shuffling the cards.

Frowning, he closed the door. "Coffee?"

"Sounds good. Got any of Lianne's apple cake around?"

Apple cake?

"She keeps it over in that cabinet." Tony pointed.

Hell, he'd barely been able to find the coffee. And she hadn't offered him anything but a cup of coffee—in the office—since the night of the brownies. He put a mug on the table and slid the sugar bowl within Tony's reach. "Spend a lot of time here?"

"A fair amount, lately."

Earlier, when he'd left the bunkhouse, Tony hadn't been his usual self. "You knew Lianne was going out tonight." *And decided to take pity on me.*

He didn't need to see the man's nod to know he'd called it right.

Well, he didn't need the sympathy. He was doing fine with the idea of Lianne being out with someone else. It was also fine that they never spent much time together in the evenings unless they had something to discuss—which they then discussed in the office.

He looked at Tony, who had patiently continued to shuffle the cards in his gnarled hands as he sat watching him.

"*Fine.* Let's have some of that apple cake."

It would be nice to play cards instead of sitting there drinking coffee by himself…in one hell of a quiet kitchen.

He found the cake and a couple of plates. "Who's dealing?"

Tony had barely finished passing out the cards when headlamps outside lit up the driveway. The old man's hands stilled as he said, "Who could that be?"

Maybe he could trust the man's innocent question. Maybe not. But he sure wouldn't make up any stories of his own again. This time when he opened the door, he didn't bother to smile.

Two new visitors stood on the doorstep.

"Did you get the word about Lianne's apple cake, too?" he asked.

"We did not," said Judge Baylor. "We saw her in town, though. Is that the cake over there? Feel free to cut me a slice."

"Me, too," said Ellamae. "Got any extra coffee?"

"Coming right up." He wasn't sure how Lianne would feel about him playing host in her kitchen, especially when they hadn't set foot in there together since they'd become housemates.

As he handed over mugs and plates, he said casually, "You saw Lianne?"

"At the Double S," the judge confirmed. "With Jack."

The guy she'd gotten all dressed up for.

"Jack is ranch manager over at Sam and Kayla's," Ellamae explained.

Lianne had mentioned her sister Kayla before.

"He sure perks right up whenever Lianne comes to visit," Ellamae added. "And of course, now she's living out here on the ranch…" She smiled down at the plate Ryan had set in front of her. "Well, that does look good."

As the other three ate Lianne's apple cake, Ryan pushed the deck of cards aside and took a long drink of coffee.

The judge sat back, thumbs under his suspenders. "How have things been going for you out here?"

"Hot enough for you, Ryan?" Ellamae asked. As with Tony's question a few minutes ago, he had some doubts about her expression.

"Fine," he said. "Just fine."

"Delighted to hear it." His cake finished, the judge took a toothpick from his pocket, stuck it in his mouth and looked Ryan over. "I thought I might've had a visit from you by now, but we haven't seen you around Town Hall."

"Or anywhere in town," Ellamae said. "And it's about time you got out a little, introduced yourself to folks."

"Had a meal at the Double S," the judge put in.

"I've been there," Tony said. "They've got some great food and even better desserts."

"They do," Ellamae agreed. "Which reminds me...Dori's doing the pastries for the party at the community center. It's next Saturday, to celebrate Memorial Day and school letting out." She smiled at Ryan. "It's the perfect opportunity to meet folks."

A kids' party at the local community center? There was nothing he'd like less. "Well, thanks, but—"

"Practically all the folks in town will be there," she added.

"As long as they're over the age of twenty-one," the judge clarified.

An adults-only party at the community center. Even that didn't sound like something to interest him.

All three of his unexpected guests sat staring at him.

He shrugged and borrowed Lianne's line. "I'll think about it."

Chapter Ten

Lianne eased the front door closed behind her and leaned back against it. She pressed her palms to the door panels as if that would keep her guilt outside. Guilt for so quickly saying good-night to Jack and leaving his car.

On her past visits to Flagman's Folly, she had gone out with Kayla and Sam's ranch foreman for coffee or dessert. Though she liked the man, she didn't want to encourage him and had made it clear that she was in a committed relationship with Mark. Or so she had thought at the time.

She and Jack met casually—that was all.

Before she had left the house, Ryan had suggested they do that, too.

As if.

When Jack had driven up to the house, she had noted all the dark windows. No lights shone from the living room or from Ryan's room upstairs. Now she could see the kitchen at the far end of the hall was dark, too.

But halfway down that hall, a light burned in her office—a lamp she had turned off before leaving the room for the day. No question about who had turned it back on and who had to be in the office now.

The question was, *why* was he in her office?

She made her way down the hall and stopped in the doorway. He stood behind her desk. Across the top, he had spread the contents of a file. Her stomach tightened as her suspicion rose.

He looked up. "You're home early."

She nodded. "How's everything?"

"Fine. Have a nice night?"

"Lovely." Moving closer to the desk, she saw the plans for phase two of the school. "Can I help you with something?"

He gestured at the drawings. "I was just taking a look. This will be an impressive project when it's all done."

She nodded. They had talked about the second phase, but she had never brought out the plans. There hadn't been a need to, when those were for the future and he would only supervise the project for a few weeks.

He rolled up the drawings and returned them to the drawer with the others. "We had some company while you were gone."

"We did? Who?"

"Tony, for one. Although I got the idea he's a regular here."

"I like a friendly chat once in a while." She and Tony talked about the school, of course, but she enjoyed the break to talk about things outside the ranch, too.

That was exactly what Ryan had been pushing for—with him.

No. She wasn't going anywhere with him, not when she still didn't trust him to keep their conversations on neutral topics. Not when she couldn't trust herself.

Hadn't she told him much more than she should have the day they hiked the trail? She needed to stay away from personal issues with Ryan. From telling him about her past. From Ryan himself.

And that was exactly why she had gone out with Jack tonight.

Dinner with him hadn't been a much bigger step than one of their dessert dates—unless you counted the fact that she'd accepted that dinner invitation as the means to avoid thinking of another man.

They hadn't made it past the appetizers before her mind raced right back to the ranch.

"You said, 'Tony, for one,'" she repeated. "Who else stopped in?"

"Ellamae and Judge Baylor. They were telling me there's a party at the community center next week. We should go."

Suspicion flared again. "I don't think attending a party together is quite the same thing as a couple of working buddies going out for coffee, do you?"

"It depends on the party. Practically all the folks in town will be at this one. I see it as a business function, a good chance to do some public relations work for the school."

And a good chance to show everyone, but especially Ryan, how well she could handle that part of her job.

He did seem very businesslike tonight. No smiling. No flirting. No attempts to get closer. No touching...

Still, uneasiness ran through her. She shrugged and said finally, "It does sound like a good PR opportunity." Through the thin fabric of her evening bag, she held on to the hard rectangle of her cell phone and considered.

They could keep things businesslike. Professional. They could keep their hands off each other and themselves to themselves. And at the Flagman's Folly Community Center...in the middle of a crowd...what could happen?

She lifted her chin. "A business function?"

"Right."

"A simple night out together?"

He nodded. "And a chance to get to know each other better."

"Like when you go to the bar with Tony and the cowboys?"

"Yeah. Just like that."

"And 'just like that' doesn't involve kissing, does it?"

When his eyes went wide, she couldn't keep from laughing.

"No, it damn well doesn't." One side of his mouth went up in a smile. "So, what do you say?"

ALL WEEK LONG, he'd looked forward to this night.

All week long, Lianne had kept reminding him this was a business deal. A chance to get to know one another.

Tables had been set at the back of the Flagman's Folly Community Center, filled with food and drinks. Most of the food had long ago disappeared, but there was still plenty of punch left. Lianne edged around the dance floor and headed toward the tables.

Ryan followed.

He couldn't have described one blamed thing in the room, even after hours spent in the place. He'd been too focused on Lianne. Tonight she'd dressed up for *him*. He couldn't help the swelling of pride in his chest—or the sudden tightness in his jeans.

Her ruffled blouse hid the curves he'd seen in the bathroom mirror and in the yard the morning she'd gone through her exercise routine. But the color of the blouse brought out the blue of her eyes—a trade-off he had no trouble accepting.

As tired as he'd felt from a long day and a longer week, the sight of her colorful skirt flipping around her knees energized him enough to make him hurry across the room behind her. Made him fool enough to act as if he were a sugar-craving filly and she held a sugar cube on her palm, just out of reach.

Out of *his* reach, for sure.

He slowed to a crawl and, this time, gave himself the reminder.

Business.

Hell, Caleb wasn't here tonight—wasn't even in town—to see what his new foreman got up to. But word would get back to him if that foreman did something inappropriate with the project manager at the Memorial Day party.

Ryan had his reputation to protect. And Lianne's.

Double the reason to be on his best behavior.

Lianne scooped punch, filling several plastic glasses. He frowned and then saw Ellamae and Roselynn had just come up to the drinks table.

From the other direction, Lianne's sister and brother-in-law approached. When Lianne had introduced Kayla and Sam earlier, Sam had made a point of saying they had a son on the way.

Another month or so yet, he had guessed, which Lianne later confirmed.

"We're heading out," Sam said now.

"Are you okay?" Lianne asked Kayla.

"Yes. Just tired."

"Better get her home," Ellamae said.

"And to bed," Roselynn added.

"That boy of yours, too." Ellamae again.

"I'm planning to," Sam agreed. "Ready, Kayla?"

"Yes. I'll text you tomorrow."

Kayla said this last bit to Lianne, who had missed most of the rapid-fire conversation. He frowned, watching her say goodbye to her family.

"Well," Ellamae said to him, "I'm glad your thinking brought you here tonight. I thought it might. Having a good time?"

"Yeah." And he was.

"I thought that, too." She grinned. "Told you this would be a good chance for you."

He narrowed his eyes.

"To talk up the school," she added.

He nodded shortly. Her sharp-eyed stare must have missed the downside of the evening.

A few times when he and Lianne had been able to talk to some of the folks in the crowded room, he'd seen how she struggled to follow conversations, just as she had a minute ago. Maybe when things like that happened, she shrugged them off. Maybe she took them in stride. Yet the times when her eyes had met his afterward, he'd seen something he couldn't quite figure out.

Ellamae and Roselynn walked off. Kayla and Sam had already crossed the room. He turned back to Lianne.

She stood alone by the punch table, staring off toward the doorway Kayla and Sam had just gone through. Or maybe at the couple dancing. Or just into space.

He couldn't figure that out, either, but he had a feeling when she looked at him again, he'd see that same damn look in her eyes. And he didn't know what to do about it.

He ran his free hand through his hair, turned to toss his empty punch cup away, and turned back.

Lianne hadn't moved.

Damn the best behavior. He grabbed her hand.

She looked up at him, her brow creased.

Before he could decide if he'd made a wise move—and he probably hadn't—before he could wonder if she'd want to dance with him—and she certainly wouldn't—before he could change his mind…he had stepped into the flow of dancers.

And the DJ had changed the music.

The beat had gone from loud, frenetic rock with a heavy bass to a slow ease-them-out-the-door ballad. He stood in the middle of the dance floor with Lianne, who couldn't hear the singer's voice.

Stepping in close, he wrapped his free arm around her. With his chin nearly brushing the top of her head, he smiled.

Just what were the chances she'd let him lead?

BUSINESS, LIANNE REMINDED HERSELF.

But how could she think about that when Ryan had his arm wrapped around her? When he wore a Western shirt that made his hazel eyes so blue?

He shifted the hand he held around her waist. She looked up.

"You okay?" he asked.

Now was the time to step away. To make it clear this was strictly business.

But she had come here tonight to show him—and everyone—how well she could handle herself. How could she let him think she couldn't manage something as simple as a dance?

"Yes," she said, looking down, using the sight of his broad, solid chest to help her focus on controlling her breath the way she did with her yoga postures.

She had already fumbled a couple of times tonight, had gotten lost in conversations, had struggled to read more than a few people. It happened.

But it had happened much more often than usual, because she'd been too aware of Ryan watching her. Assessing her?

His fingers moved restlessly at the small of her back. Slowly, she raised her gaze.

He smiled.

She had no control over the way her heart fluttered at the change that brought to his face. With all the time they'd spent arguing, going toe to toe, she hadn't seen a smile like that often. But when she had, she'd noted every step of the transformation, just as she noted it now. The tiny grooves dimpled the skin on either side of his mouth. The cleft in his chin deepened. The skin around his eyes crinkled.

She wanted him to smile that way again, for her alone.

But if he did, she would never be able to resist…anything.

Business, she told herself yet again.

She closed her eyes, took a deep breath and inhaled the delicious scent of his aftershave. On their ride here, she had added that scent to her mental wish list.

Cradled in his arms, she knew she'd already gotten the wish she had made last week.

All through dinner at the Double S with another man, her thoughts had drifted back to the ranch. To Ryan. He was the man she wanted to be with. The man she really wanted to get to know.

He stopped moving. She opened her eyes and looked across the empty dance floor.

Then she glanced up at him. He was smiling down at her again.

Business, she warned herself.

Or pleasure?

THANK HIS LUCKY STARS, she'd taken him to her bed.

His suggestion to go to the party hadn't been designed to get him here. He'd swear that on his custom-made saddle.

But after their turn on the community center's dance floor and their good-night interlude in the living room, he'd been more than ready to follow when she led him toward the stairs.

Now he was ready to kiss her, to hold her, to go on to whatever happened from there—and he wanted everything to go right.

She wanted to chat.

He bit back a smile. At least they weren't quite talking about the weather, the way she had the day of their hike.

So far she had covered her sister's family, which was what had brought her to Flagman's Folly originally, her previous trips here, how much the environment had surprised her and how she liked to do her yoga at sunrise.

Oh, yeah, on that one. He shifted on his elbow and smiled down at her. He reckoned her chatting came from nerves, and her nerves came from having some experience but not enough to make her treat this like just another roll in the hay. He appreciated the honor.

She wasn't just another woman for him, either. The thought caused a funny tight feeling in his chest.

"I had only seen pictures of the Southwest before I came to visit Kayla and Becky," she went on. "Other than cities, I'd expected to find nothing here but desert. Do you remember the trail?"

As if he could forget. He nodded.

"I've gone back there a couple of times. We didn't climb high enough—" She paused, as if recalling what had ended their day, then rushed on. "Not far past the picnic bench, there's a bridge that spans the stream. On the opposite bank, there's an open space among the trees. It catches the light when the sun comes up."

She laughed softly, that throaty chuckle he'd learned to look forward to hearing.

"These will sound like the worst clichés you've ever heard," she went on, "but the sun rising in a place like that really makes it feel like a shrine. Or a temple. And pine needles really do make a soft carpet. It's so beautiful there."

He ran his finger along her soft cheek. "You're beautiful."

Her eyes gleamed. "It's quiet there, too."

"Quiet?"

"I know. That sounds funny to you. I can't hear, so what do I know about quiet. But…I use my eyes all day long. To read signs and lips and faces. To catch movements and gestures so I'm aware of what's happening around me. And for reading and the computer, of course. Sometimes all that visual stimulation wears me out."

Smiling, he ran his fingertips along her jawline. "I'm hoping to wear you out. But with another kind of stimulation."

He kissed her as thoroughly and completely as he knew how. And then he went back for more.

A while later he rolled over and reached up to turn off the bedside lamp. She put her hand on his arm. When he looked over his shoulder at her, she shook her head. He shrugged, rolled back again and took up where they'd left off.

It had been a long time since he'd made love with the lights on, but he wasn't about to let that stop him.

A buzzing noise suddenly filled the room.

Lianne looked up, a smile on her lips. He lowered his head and took her mouth again. This kiss went on and on.

So did the buzzing.

He brushed his jaw lightly against her petal-smooth cheek, as if he could brush the noise away.

It kept going. What the hell *was* it?

He raised his head, followed the sound across the room and found the source. Her cell phone, its screen brightly lit, nearly danced as it vibrated on the dresser.

Lianne hadn't noticed. He ignored it, smiled and kissed her again. The text or the email, whatever it was, would get saved.

The phone continued to vibrate, one message following another following another.

He slid his hand from her cheek to her jaw to her shoulder. Then he froze.

Damn. That thought he'd had—*Lianne hadn't noticed.*

It had flashed into his mind, and he'd just as quickly let it go by.

He rested his palm on the pillow beside her head. From where she lay, she couldn't see the light of the phone's screen. From anywhere in the room, she wouldn't hear the vibration of the plastic casing against the wood of the dresser.

He couldn't ignore the buzzing any longer. He couldn't *not* give her the option of answering the damned thing. Of jumping on the excuse to call things—call *them*—to a halt, if she wanted one.

And it seemed she did. When he pointed, she turned her head and saw the light from the phone. She slipped from the bed and padded across the room.

As she picked up the phone, he watched her reflection in the mirror over the dresser. Saw her brow crease while she scanned the first message. Watched her thumbs tapping keys and assumed she went on to the next message and the next.

And the next.

She would barely pause at the end of a series of taps, and the phone would vibrate yet again. Her fingers worked furiously as she started to key in one response after another.

She hadn't looked at him once. He might as well not have been in the room.

Before tonight he had seen her turn her head away to end a conversation she didn't want to have with him.

Now she focused on the cell phone, just as effectively shutting him out.

Maybe those nerves had gotten to her. Maybe she'd had second thoughts. Fourth or fifth thoughts. Maybe even before this, her chattering had come from a need to avoid something she no longer wanted. In that case, no matter what he tried, things wouldn't go the way he'd hoped.

He got to his feet. Picked up his boots. Waited.

Her gaze stayed on the phone. Her thumbs flew over the keys. Her brow stayed creased and her back remained facing him.

Right.

He left her room and headed for his own, leaving his desires behind. All for the best. He had never forced a woman to spend time with him, and he sure as hell had never played games to get one into bed.

She's not just any woman.

The thought chased him into his room.

He looked at the photo frame on the dresser. All this week, he hadn't given a thought to his wife *or* his son.

He tossed his boots into the closet, yanked his shirt from his jeans and shook his head. His trip to Lianne's bed had worked out just the way it should have.

But damn, what *could* have happened still had him hard and breathing heavy.

Or…*would* anything have happened? Was this still fun and games for Lianne, the way it had been in the beginning?

Had she wanted the lights left on so she could make an easy escape? Would she have stopped things just as they got interesting, the way she had that day on the trail when he'd kissed her?

And damn it all, why had he forgotten his goal, put aside his need to rebuild his reputation, just to let himself get caught up in her stories again?

Chapter Eleven

Apparently, Ryan had found it easy to replace one appetite with another. Lianne found him in the kitchen with a mug of coffee and a plate of pie on the table in front of him.

"Did you save me a piece?" she asked.

His eyebrows shot up. She had surprised him. Maybe her bedroom slippers hadn't made enough noise for him to hear her in the hall. "I'm sorry about this." She gestured with the phone in her hand.

He nodded.

She rested her shoulder against the doorframe. "Kayla's husband, Sam, texted me, and we went back and forth for a while. Then I heard from his mom, Sharleen. And after that, finally, Kayla herself. She's at the hospital."

He put down the mug he'd just lifted. "Everything okay?"

Her heart fluttered at his obvious concern. "Yes. But evidently my nephew's getting restless."

"She's having him now?"

"No. They're sending her home again, but she needs to take it easy. They want her to get closer to her due date."

He shifted in his chair and pushed the plate away. "Guess she knows the routine."

"Why would she…? Oh. Becky." She shook her head. "No, we're sort of a complicated family. The baby is Kayla's first."

If he had asked a question, if he hadn't dropped his gaze, if he hadn't reached for his fork again, she might have explained.

If she hadn't had to track him down, she wouldn't be standing here leaning against the doorframe. She stood upright. He hadn't looked over at her again. The first sight of his midnight snack should have clued her in.

"I'm ready for bed." Only as the words left her mouth did she realize how he might take the statement. But he didn't react to the double meaning, just nodded and stabbed another piece of pie.

She turned and left the room.

Now her heart thumped painfully. Her eyes blurred. Despite her determination not to think of what had happened between them, the thoughts came. Just a few minutes ago he had kissed her nearly senseless. His hands had touched her, stroked her, as though she were something delicate and easily broken...

Or *already* broken? Was that why he had taken such care with her?

She almost missed a step on the stairs.

As she went up to the second floor, she felt no footsteps behind her. When she looked back from the doorway of her bedroom, the hall was deserted. He hadn't followed. And she shouldn't, *couldn't,* have expected him to.

Why would he come after her now when he had been so quick to use her texts as an excuse to stop kissing her and leave her bedroom? When he so obviously preferred pie to...to...*passion.*

The comparison did the trick, allowing her to laugh despite the threatening tears.

That was what she got for falling for his "get to know you" line. For taking the risk of mixing pleasure into their business relationship. Clearly, he had gotten to spend enough time with her to know he wasn't interested.

And she needed to get her job done.

An impossible goal, maybe, with Ryan still her supervisor, working beside her every day. With Ryan such a distraction, she found it hard to focus on spreadsheets and schedules.

How would she manage to concentrate at all now, with her memories of what had happened between them tonight... *before* the texts?

She should have known better than to get involved with him at all. Hadn't she learned her lesson in Chicago?

Two steps took her into her bedroom. She turned back and smacked the door shut.

LIANNE TOOK THE chair from the corner of the bedroom and set it beside the bed.

"I'm so glad to see you." Smiling, Kayla pushed the sheet aside. *"I can use someone to talk to. Sam and Sharleen already had a fit because I wouldn't sleep in this morning."*

"So I heard." She had seen Sam and his mother downstairs.

"Of course, I won't do anything against my doctor's orders. But he hasn't said anything about full bed rest."

Lianne smiled, happy to see for herself what Kayla had texted last night: everything was fine. She could just imagine how bored her normally active sister must feel.

"And I'm doing great. Just tired. I was so tired on our way out of the community center last night I forgot to sign."

"Don't worry about that. And take a break from it now. I'm only a few feet away." She scooted the chair a little closer. "Sorry to get here so early, but I wanted to see you face-to-face."

She could only hope her voice sounded natural. Her desire to see Kayla had been matched by her desire *not* to see Ryan at all this morning. She had lingered upstairs in her room until he had walked past the barn on his way to the bunkhouse. Cowardly, yes. But she hadn't felt ready to face him.

As soon as she had showered and dressed, she'd gone into town to the Double S for breakfast. And now she had come here.

"I'll be back in two minutes," Kayla said. "Then you can fill me in."

Lianne slumped in her chair. Maybe this hadn't been such a good idea after all. But she couldn't have stayed at the ranch house all day, attempting to work but wondering when Ryan would make a sudden appearance in her office doorway. Wondering, yet again, how glad he had felt for the excuse to escape from her last night.

Part of her wished she would never have to go back there, never have to face the truth.

Last night *she had taken him to her bedroom*.

What had she been thinking? She should have listened to herself the day they had hiked up the trail and he'd kissed her.

Hot or not, with all his micromanaging, he had already proven how little respect he had for her abilities.

And she had sworn off men who wouldn't treat her as an equal.

Kayla padded into the room again, climbed onto the bed and adjusted the pillow she had propped up behind her, as if settling in for a long conversation.

Lianne shifted in her chair. She couldn't dump everything on Kayla now. In fact, maybe she could help her. "Since school's out, how about I borrow Becky overnight? It's lonely out at the ranch, and I could use some company."

"You're welcome to take her anytime—you know that,"

Kayla said. "But she's already arranged to have her friend sleep over here tonight."

"I saw P.J. downstairs." She knew the little boy and his family from previous visits. "I'll take him along with me, too. Can you clear it with his mom?"

Kayla smiled. "You must be desperate to want to take them both."

If she only knew.... "No, I'm just thinking it would give Sharleen a break."

That was true enough. But her request had had nothing to do with being lonely on the ranch. How could she be lonely? She talked with Tony often and made her daily trips out to the construction site. And once she had agreed to go to the party at the community center, Ryan had found more reasons to come into the office. She couldn't deal with that now. Not after last night.

No, taking Becky and P.J. out to the ranch had nothing to do with loneliness.

She glanced at Kayla, who sat doing some thinking of her own. She could almost see the gears turning in her sister's head. Finally, Kayla said, "That's actually a great idea. Sharleen would never say she needed the rest, but we had a late night last night. Becky wears her out, and she's going to need all her energy if she and Sam want me to stay in bed all day. "You're sure you don't mind taking P.J., too?"

"The more the merrier." And the more help she would have in resisting Ryan. "Why don't you make the call so I can go tell the kids about the change of plans?"

"Okay—*if* you talk to me afterward."

Lianne sighed. Kayla had always been good for a bit of sisterly blackmail.

"Come on, big sis. I saw you on that dance floor last night."

Heat flooded her face. "I thought you'd left."

"I needed to make a quick restroom stop. It's a long ride from the community center to home. By the way," she added, "Ellamae's on her way over. And you know what that means."

They both did. She'd better start talking—fast.

She loved Tess's aunt. But Ellamae had been at the community center. After Ryan had led her off the dance floor, she had seen Ellamae's big grin. The woman would want to be filled in, too. Just as Kayla did.

"Sharleen said she's bringing breakfast rolls from the Whistlestop." Kayla grinned. "So what's it going to be? Talk to me? Or face a *real* inquisition?"

Sighing, Lianne picked up the cordless phone from the nightstand near Kayla and handed it to her.

ALL HELL HAD broken loose in the kitchen.

Ryan had come by the house more times than he should have today, but he was determined to keep their working relationship working as well as possible, all things considered. Fool that he was, he'd already lost his determination to stop thinking about last night.

Luckily, thinking and doing were two different things.

On his first trip back to the house, the empty space in the driveway had told him Lianne was not to be found. That state of affairs had continued all day.

Now the car sat parked in its regular space again, the kitchen was in chaos, and he still didn't see her.

He froze with his hand on the door he had just opened and with his boots planted on the porch. The noise blasting at him from inside the room could have knocked a bull rider out of his saddle before he'd even gotten clear of the chute.

On the counter, a radio with the bass control cranked to high boomed something with a heavy drumbeat trying to outplay screaming guitars. Caleb's daughter, Nate, sang at the top of her lungs into an invisible microphone.

From somewhere beneath the kitchen table, a dog barked.

At the table, a small boy and girl laughed and screeched over the game board spread in front of them.

Damn. His stomach tensed and his chest compressed and he had to struggle to take a breath.

Finally, he saw Lianne, with her back to them all, rummaging in the refrigerator.

Easing the door closed behind him, he stepped into the kitchen. He rubbed the back of his hand across his chin and wondered how the hell he was going to get across the room alive—and without any of them noticing as he passed through.

The last thing he wanted was to be around a bunch of kids. Then he took a closer look at the pair playing at the table and saw things he wished *he* hadn't noticed.

The little girl who knelt on the ladder-back chair at the table was the one he'd almost hit with his truck. The boy in the chair beside hers appeared to be just the age Billy would be now.

And the game they were playing looked all too familiar.

Got to get out of this room.

Too late. Nate spotted him standing there, feet frozen to the floor. Abruptly, she stopped screeching and smacked her palm against the top of the radio. The noise level in the room decreased by about eighty percent. The music still pounded in his head.

"Hey, Ryan!" Nate yelled. "Did you know my daddy's coming home tomorrow?"

The pounding in his head increased. Right now he couldn't think about Caleb's return. But he nodded in response.

Nate swept the air, gesturing toward the table. "That's

P.J.—he's my best friend's brother—and that's Becky. She doesn't talk, so I'll have to help you when you want to talk to her." She stopped to gulp a breath and then rushed on. "Guess what. We're having a sleepover and you're just in time for the barbecue!"

He got a stranglehold on the brim of the Stetson he'd removed at the door. "Well, thanks, but—"

Lianne slammed the refrigerator door closed and turned their way, her arms filled with bottles and jars of ketchup, mustard and what looked like pickle relish. Their gazes met, and she tightened her hold on the containers.

"Lianne!" Nate said. "Look who's here."

"I see." She lifted the condiments like a shield and looked as though she wanted to run from the room, too.

"Ryan's having supper with us," Nate said.

"Is he?"

"Yeah. I can carry those outside." She reached to take the bottles and jars.

"Great." Lianne set everything in a wicker basket and handed it over. "Thank you."

Nate left the room, letting the door slam behind her. The kid—P.J.—followed. He carried a package of napkins and a plastic cup under each arm like footballs. Just the way Billy did.

"Here," Lianne said, not meeting his eyes.

Before he could protest, she shoved a plastic-wrapped platter of hamburger patties at him. He grabbed it with his free hand just as she turned away again. If he hadn't closed his fingers around the edge of the platter, the burgers would have landed on the floor.

She turned to her niece. The two of them started to talk, their hands flying, their faces alight, their mouths not saying a word. Not a whisper broke the silence…until

Lianne laughed, that soft, throaty sound he'd last heard in her bedroom.

Before he could think straight, he had barreled through the doorway and found himself on the back porch again. And there he stood holding the danged platter of raw meat.

He didn't want to stay for supper. He didn't want to be there at all. Lianne didn't want him around, either. Her actions and expression made that all too clear.

They also made him suddenly downright determined to stick around.

RYAN HELD HIS hand over the grill. The charcoal ought to be good and ready, since it burned at a heat level equal to the irritation in his gut.

Not long after he'd set the platter on the shelf attached to the grill, he'd begun wishing he'd stuck to his first reaction and run right through the kitchen in the other direction— upstairs to his room.

The little boy stood near his elbow, close enough to make it impossible for Ryan to ignore him, let alone to pretend he didn't exist. For now, at least, the kid seemed to have run out of questions to ask. Without blinking an eye, he watched every move of the spatula as if he were starving—or had never seen anyone make such a mess of flipping burgers.

Why couldn't the kid have stayed on the other side of the yard with Lianne and the girls, continuing their silent conversation and leaving him manning the grill?

How did he get drafted into the job, anyhow? Carrying the platter out to the yard shouldn't have automatically nominated him as chief cook. He slapped the spatula on the grill and flipped another burger. It fell through the rack and onto the coals below.

Three down. At this rate, they'd all have to turn vegetarian for the evening.

"Do you need some help?" the boy beside him asked.

"No, I'm good," he said.

Your nose is gonna grow like Pinocchio's, Daddy!

Billy had always shouted that when he suspected a lie. And he'd just now told a heck of a whopper.

The five-year-old reminded him too much of his own son. The little girl had run up to join them and now stood silently with her silver-gray eyes trained on him, too. Again he kicked himself for not having turned tail and run.

Lianne sauntered over to them. "Are we having a problem here?" She pointed to the burgers that had fallen through the rack.

First the kid, now her. He ground his molars and fibbed again, "No, things are great." He gestured toward the dog that was never more than a foot from the girl. "Those are for Pirate."

Lianne bit the corner of her lip, probably to hide a smile.

P.J. tugged on Becky's sleeve. When he'd gotten her attention, he pointed to the fallen burgers, too, and then moved his free hand—all his fingertips touching—toward the dog. "For Pirate." He clapped his hand over his eye.

The sign stood for the dog's name, which Becky had apparently given to the mutt the minute she'd seen him. The dog had a patch of dark fur around his eye; it was a nice piece of logic.

Kids that age had plenty of smarts....

Becky grinned and wiggled her upright hands in the air.

"She's clapping," P.J. told him.

"Pirate's a lucky boy," Lianne said, looking into the grill.

He frowned. Returning his attention to his task, he flipped another burger. Carefully. He'd already made enough for the mutt.

"We'll be eating soon," she added. *"Time to go wash your hands."*

The two younger ones scampered away, the dog in pursuit. Nate took off after them. Ryan was left alone with the rest of the sizzling burgers. And with Lianne.

She stood staring at him as steadily as the kids had done. "Let me know if you plan to do any of the cooking for the scouts' campfire. I'll increase the food budget."

"Very funny." He transferred the cooked burgers to the platter she held out to him.

"What's not funny is the way you're behaving."

He raised his brows. "I can't help the way I cook." But that wasn't what she meant, and he knew it.

"You can help how you're talking—or I should say not talking—to the kids."

He shrugged, not intending to tell her he wanted nothing to do with the kids, especially the younger ones.

P.J. overflowed with the same little-boy enthusiasm his son had shown. He had the same habit of asking a never-ending list of questions. Even his hair, though blond instead of brown, grew in a cowlick that refused to be tamed, just as Billy's had.

And Becky—

"If you didn't feel sociable, you could have gone on your way. You didn't have to accept Nate's invitation."

"That last part's true." Though he hadn't actually received—or accepted—an invitation. More like Nate had taken for granted he'd stay to supper. "But the rest has nothing to do with being sociable or not. I was paying attention to my cooking."

She glanced quickly at the grill and shook her head. "I suppose that's a good thing. I don't want to think about what would happen if you didn't focus."

She looked up, her eyes sparkling, her cheeks flushed a pale pink. "As I was saying—"

"Yeah. Focus." Any determination he'd ever mustered

to keep his distance went up in a puff of charcoal-scented smoke. He took the platter from her, set it on the shelf and turned back. "Want to know what I'm focusing on now? Read my lips."

Chapter Twelve

As Ryan leaned closer, Lianne tensed. Ever since last night, she had reminded herself of the list of reasons she needed to stay away from him. All the reasons she needed to be strong. But she couldn't let him see her run.

He slipped his arm around her waist and rested his free hand against her cheek.

A warmth spread through her, one she couldn't blame on the heat from the grill.

He held her closer, the way he had on the dance floor. She braced her hands on his biceps, the way she had in her bedroom last night.

And she slipped free of his arm and stepped away.

"Hey—" His gaze darted over her shoulder.

That was enough to tell her the kids had returned to the yard. Good. He would have to keep his hands to himself.

The warmth filling her had nothing to do with his touch or the look in his eyes. It came from anger at what he had attempted and what she had almost let him get away with.

She had tried to talk about why he wasn't interacting with the kids. He'd wanted…to do something else.

"Interesting," she said thoughtfully.

"I'd call it more than that."

"I mean our conversation. You deliberately changed the subject, didn't you? I was pointing out how you had avoided the kids, and you used that…*maneuver* as a way to distract me."

He frowned. "It wasn't a maneuver."

She opened her mouth and snapped it shut again. She wouldn't be able to tell if her voice rose too high, and she couldn't risk the kids overhearing what she wanted to say. Hands trembling, she grabbed the platter of hamburgers from the shelf.

Pirate darted between them, his head raised to sniff the air.

"No, Pirate. Ryan has yours." She turned away.

Nate ran toward them. Behind her Becky and P.J. had climbed up to sit at the picnic table.

Ryan put his hand on her shoulder. Reluctantly, she looked back at him.

"Lianne, I don't play games."

She shrugged. His hand slipped away.

"We're starving," Nate said. "Are the hamburgers ready yet?"

She hoped her laugh didn't sound forced. "Right here. Let's go." She followed Nate to the table.

Ryan had stayed beside the grill. His hair gleamed in the sunshine. His eyes sparkled as he played with the dog. He tore a hamburger patty into bits and tossed the pieces to Pirate, who snapped them up as though he hadn't eaten in days.

Dragging her gaze away, she dropped a hamburger onto a bun and concentrated on smacking the bottom of the upended ketchup bottle. The irony of the situation didn't escape her. She had brought the kids here to help her stay away from Ryan, and here she was, annoyed because he wanted to stay away from them.

He had interacted with Nate and P.J. only when they approached him. Becky was another story. As far as she could tell, from the moment he had walked into the kitchen until now, he hadn't sent a smile, a gesture or even a glance in her niece's direction.

His attitude irritated her at the same time it stirred memories, triggering a well-known pressure in the pit of her stomach and a familiar ache in her heart. At school she didn't have to face sitting alone with people who couldn't understand her. But later, home again, there were plenty of barbecues, birthday parties, holiday dinners… She had spent too many of them sitting alone and overlooked by most of the adults and ignored by the kids, feeling as though she didn't fit in.

She didn't ever want anyone to make Becky feel that way.

Especially Ryan.

Now he approached the picnic table with Pirate trotting along beside him. The closest seat open would put him opposite her and beside Becky. Without a glance at either of them, he went to the far end of the table. Pirate put his front paws on the edge of the bench near Becky.

Her stomach churning, Lianne set the hamburger back on her plate. Ketchup oozed from around the edges, and her fingertips had left craters in the bun.

She sighed, knowing it was more than just Ryan's unwillingness to communicate that upset her.

She wanted him to care. To look at Becky and not see a less-than-perfect child. To look at *her* and not see someone less than whole. She wanted him just to accept them, as is, no expectations attached.

RYAN PUT ON a clean pair of jeans and sat on the foot of the bed to put his boots on. Every muscle in his body ached from the tension of getting through the evening before.

He should have followed his instincts and headed right upstairs instead of staying for supper. He should have come up with an excuse to leave the ranch altogether. And he sure as hell should *not* have tried to kiss Lianne again.

If he had known she would wind up throwing those accusations at him, he wouldn't have gone near her at all.

Maneuver, she'd said. He'd give her a *maneuver* she wouldn't soon forget. He'd kiss her—

"Morning."

The boot slipped from his fingers and thudded to the carpet at his feet.

The voice had come from the hall. He turned his head toward the door and saw the body that went with it— pint-sized, dressed in pajamas printed with stars and spaceships, and carrying a bed pillow.

P.J.

Other than the cowlick, the kid didn't look much like his son. But his eyes were puffy and pillow-creased, like Billy's when he first woke up. His hair went every which way, like Billy's when he first crawled out from under the covers. And that cowlick, just like Billy's, stood up on the back of his head.

The boy crossed the room and climbed up onto the bed. He settled the sheets around him to his satisfaction, then plopped the pillow onto his lap and leaned his elbows on it. "That barbecue was a long time ago. You think we'll get breakfast soon?"

He stared, trying to regain his breath and bring his thoughts back from the past. After a moment, he reached down for his fallen boot. "I don't know. Anybody up yet besides you and me?"

"Just Pirate. But he can't cook."

Right. He managed a sickly grin.

"Whatcha doin'?"

Looking down, he focused on putting his boot on. "Getting ready for work." And for the inevitable list of questions.

"Are you the boss of this ranch?"

Ha. That sure recalled him to the here and now—and the problems he faced in it. He tried to keep the sourness from his tone. "I like to think I run this place, kid, but I reckon that depends on who you ask."

"Oh." P.J. shrugged. "Did you know there's gonna be a lot of boys at this ranch soon?"

"Yes." Luckily, he wouldn't see a single one of them.

"Do *you* have any boys?"

His mouth suddenly dry, he stared at P.J. without speaking.

P.J. stared back, blue eyes unblinking, waiting for a response.

Just like Billy, trusting his daddy to have all the answers.

"I—" How could he explain to a five-year-old? "No. I don't have any boys."

"Oh." The kid rolled his eyes. "You have *girls?*" His voice dropped a few notches on the final word.

Ryan shook his head. "Don't have any of those, either. You got something against girls?"

"They think they're so smart. And they always want to be the boss."

Now, wasn't that the truth. "Like Nate?"

An emphatic nod. "And my big sister. Not the little one yet." As if Ryan had commented, he added, "Well, Becky's a girl, too, but she's okay. She can't talk, but that's okay, too. My mama says she's just like me. Do you know any signs?"

"No, I don't."

"I know lots." P.J. touched one fingertip to his cheek and twisted it. "This is *candy.* And this—" he curved his hand into a claw and dragged his fingertips down his stomach "—means *hungry.*"

Ryan nodded, trying to smile but only managing to lift one corner of his mouth.

He went over to the closet and grabbed a shirt hanging from the rod. From behind him he heard the sound of wood scraping against wood. He froze with the shirt halfway on.

"Who's this?" P.J. asked.

He slid his shirt on. Then, one by one, he snapped the snaps. Finally, he turned back into the room.

Over by the dresser, P.J. stood holding the picture frame, gazing down at the photo Ryan hadn't looked at in nearly a year.

He cleared his throat. "That's my family."

P.J. frowned, squinting with his entire face just the way Billy did when something puzzled him. "But you said you didn't *have* any boys."

"He… He's not with me anymore."

"Oh." He nodded. "You mean he's in heaven?"

He took a deep breath and let it out again. "Yeah, he's in heaven."

"Like my daddy. Well, my old daddy. I have a new daddy now." P.J. stood the frame on the dresser. He crossed the room again and dragged his pillow from the bed. "I'm going downstairs. Maybe it's time for breakfast."

Ryan watched him leave and then sat on the edge of the bed. He kept his gaze from the picture frame but couldn't keep the questions from ringing in his head, the same unanswered questions, like the nightmares, he'd carried with him from Montana.

The accident *had* told him one thing—how quickly disasters could happen, with lives ending in an instant. Families lost in the space of a breath.

He let himself look at Jan and Billy. Then he tore his gaze away and thought of Lianne.

I can manage this, she told him over and over again. *I can handle that. I can do my job. I don't need your help.*

Maybe. Maybe not.

Who could predict when a disaster would happen?

ON THE WAY back from town, Lianne's cell phone vibrated. Ryan's name sprang into her thoughts—ridiculous, as he didn't even have her phone number.

The text had come from Caleb. He and Tess wanted to meet with them both at the Double S for dinner. Just what she needed.

Breakfast with the kids had helped distract her from her irritation with Ryan.

Last night he had disappeared after helping to bring everything in from the backyard, and they hadn't seen him again.

This morning he never came near the house at all.

Considering his usual pattern, she had thought they would see him at least once before she left to take the kids home—as if he would have wanted to say goodbye to any of them.

She glanced at the clock on the dashboard before getting out of the car and slamming the door closed. He wouldn't be able to avoid her much longer. She just hoped she would be able to control herself until after the night was over.

The minute she saw him at the kitchen table, she had to fight to swallow the things she wanted to say.

She managed a civil question. "Did you hear from Caleb?"

"Yep. I was just headed up to shower. Get the kids home okay?"

If he hadn't said that, she might have been able to last longer. But he had, and she couldn't. "Ryan, why wouldn't you talk with Becky last night? You didn't have to know how to sign. You could have pointed, gestured, smiled— done *anything* to acknowledge her."

He rose from his seat, his thumbs in his belt loops.

His good ol' gunslinger-at-the-ready position.

It made her ready for a shoot-out with him. It made her see

red. It made her feel—as he would probably say—downright furious. All the emotion she had bottled up from the night before—the weeks before—poured out. "I know you've got issues with me because I can't hear. I can deal with that. But for Pete's sake, she's a five-year-old. An innocent child. She can't help that she can't talk to you. And knowing she's deaf shouldn't make you avoid her like she's got the plague."

"I didn't."

"You did." She clutched a handful of her hair, took a deep breath and let it out again. "All right. You're not deaf. I guess it's too much for you ever to understand. But can't you see how she feels when people pretend she's not there—even when she's right in front of them?"

"Left out."

"What?" She couldn't have read those words on his lips.

He moved toward her, as if he thought she couldn't see his mouth from across the room. "Left out," he repeated.

She stared. She *had* read him correctly.

"Irritated," he addcd.

She blinked.

"Frustrated."

She took another deep breath. "You *do* know."

"I've been there. Last night in the kitchen. Watching you sign with her when I didn't know a word you were saying. Out in the yard, seeing you all talking together."

Her throat tightened at this first indication that he might care. "You could have talked to her through me. Becky's comfortable with having an interpreter."

"After what happened on Signal Street, I wanted to apologize to her. Directly."

"You could have taken me aside after dinner and explained."

"Maybe." He shrugged, looked away, looked back again. "Was there ever a time when she could hear?"

When she wasn't less than perfect? Her heart ached. She shook her head. "She was born profoundly deaf."

"Then she doesn't hear birds singing? Or the voices of the kids she plays with?"

She shook her head again.

"She even misses out on hearing her dog bark?"

"She doesn't hear Pirate, either. But she doesn't miss his bark. She doesn't 'miss' any of those things. Someone born hearing who becomes deaf later on has a memory of sounds. Becky doesn't. She can't miss something she's never known."

"And how do you feel?"

She curled her fingers into fists.

Finally.

They had been tiptoeing around her situation since the day they had met. Sometimes her deafness still didn't seem to matter to him. That couldn't make up for the times when he let his doubts and resistance show.

Even if last night had ended differently, they would have arrived at this point eventually. Inevitably.

And here they were, face-to-face in a situation she had encountered all through her life. Having to tell about her deafness. Having to explain how she managed without hearing. Instead of happiness that he might have some respect for her abilities, she was again forced to confront a hearing man who focused on what she *couldn't* do.

She had hoped to get beyond that with this man.

"I told you I can't hear anyone's voice," she reminded him. "I can hear some sounds. Loud thunder. Drums. An explosion. Even with music, no matter how loud, I don't hear the words clearly. I feel the vibrations." She thought of the night he'd held her on the dance floor, when she hadn't needed anything to be able to follow his steps. Then she pushed the memory away.

"Ryan, I've been deaf my entire life. Like Becky, I don't miss what I've never heard. And—" she brought her fists down hard, emotion adding emphasis to the sign "—I *can* do anything anyone else can."

He looked at her for a long moment. She wanted to cry. Or run. She wouldn't do either.

Finally, he shook his head. "That wasn't what I was getting at when I asked."

"Then what?"

"I meant, how do you feel when people pretend you're not there?"

Didn't he always ask questions designed to throw her? She crossed her arms, cradling her elbows in the palms of her hands. He spoke again, preventing her from looking away.

"How did you feel at Becky's age?" he persisted. "Irritated?"

"Yes."

"Frustrated?"

"Very."

"Left out?"

Her fingers tightened. "Yes."

"Lonely?"

Her throat tightened, too. She could only nod. He did understand the feelings. He *did* care. And maybe, if he could understand her, he could eventually accept why she cared so much about being treated like everyone else.

She took a deep, calming breath and let it out again. "Like Becky, I don't hear. But there are so many things I don't need to know *here*—" she pointed to her ear "—because I can feel them *here*." She rested her hand over her heart.

He reached across the space between them and touched

her fingers, as gently as the first time he had touched her face to wipe the pencil smudge away.

She hoped her hand could prevent him from feeling the pounding of her heart.

Could he hear it?

Surprise froze her in place. A thought like that had never occurred to her. But then, she had never been in a situation like this one…and she had never before cared about a man the way she cared about him.

He dropped his hand by his side. "I'd best go and get ready for supper."

She nodded.

It took all her willpower not to reach out to him the way he had done to her. He had taken one step closer to understanding, and she was grateful for that.

Would he continue to take steps until they met each other halfway?

AFTER THEIR QUIET ride to town, Ryan would have liked some time alone to talk with Lianne, but she went through the door of the local café without a backward glance.

He followed, taking stock of the room, from the sombreros on the wall to the unvarnished tables and chairs. With luck, the Southwestern theme of the Double S would carry through to their menu.

They had arrived early. Caleb and his wife weren't there yet. His mother-in-law and her sister were seated at a table near the front of the café next to the window looking onto Signal Street.

Roselynn smiled and waved them over.

Ellamae pointed out where they should sit. She put him at one end of the table with Lianne at a right angle to him. All right by him.

Back at the house, it had seemed as if they'd made some

progress. Maybe she hadn't been playing games with him as he'd believed after all.

The thought made him feel better than he had in days.

He hadn't realized he was smiling until Lianne smiled at him in return. That went down well with him, too.

"We hear you're doing some good work out at the ranch," Roselynn said.

"Yeah," Ellamae put in, "Caleb's very pleased."

"That's good to hear." He meant it, more than the woman could ever know.

Nate entered the café and headed right for their table. Ellamae seemed to have given up on dictating who sat where, since the girl slid onto the chair beside Lianne's all on her own. "Hi again, Lianne. Hi, Ryan. We were looking for you after lunch today before we left the ranch. What happened to you?"

"He was working, Nate," Ellamae said as if she had been there. "He's a busy man."

"Lianne's busy, too," Nate said.

"Of course she is."

Caleb and Tess arrived at the table in time to hear the exchange. "And they're going to get busier," he said, taking a seat across from Lianne.

The waitress followed, bringing two baskets of taco chips and pots of salsa. Dori, her name was, and she spent the next few minutes chatting with them. When they got around to giving their orders, Ryan watched her write them down on her pad. She kept smiling despite all the commotion at the table and Nate changing her mind three times. No matter what Lianne had told him, he still couldn't imagine how she had done a job like waitressing. He wouldn't have wanted the challenge.

"Manny will have this ready for you soon," Dori promised.

When she left to get their drinks, Lianne turned to Caleb. "What's this about getting busier?"

"I'd like to let the folks in town know about our plans for the ranch. I figure the best way to do that is to give a presentation at the next town council meeting."

"That sounds perfect," Lianne said. "It would give everyone a chance to be there."

"Yeah," Nate said, "so they can make sure it's not a *dude* ranch."

Lianne laughed. Ryan shifted in his chair.

"I'll work my magic and get it on the agenda for the next meeting," Ellamae said.

Caleb nodded. "Right. Well before the official opening."

"That sounds like good timing," Ryan said.

Caleb ran down a list of what they would want to include for the presentation.

When talk turned to additional plans for the school's operation, Ryan settled back in his seat, having a hard time focusing. Chances were he wouldn't be there to see the school open.

Being promoted to ranch foreman had put him a step closer to rebuilding his reputation and regaining Caleb's trust. Now that his boss was back, would he get to keep his title and continue to supervise the school construction?

If he did, how would that affect the situation with Lianne?

By the time they'd finished supper and said good-night to Caleb's family, he'd started wishing he could head back to Montana right now.

He and Lianne had come to town in his truck. When he opened her door, she put one foot up on the running board. Then she turned to him. "What is it?" she asked.

After he'd gone quiet at supper, she had eyed him a few times with that stare that made him think she could see more about him than he knew himself. He'd known her question was coming but didn't want to get into it with her. "What's what?"

"Don't." She shook her head impatiently. "You wouldn't even look at me again after Caleb started talking about the presentation. What's bothering you about it?"

Not the question he'd expected. He had to stop himself from smiling in relief. They would talk this out and then things would go back to normal between them. "Nothing's bothering me," he said honestly. "I've got no trouble talking to folks."

"You've got—?" Her eyes glittered in the light from the streetlamp. "Don't do that, either. Ryan, stop putting limitations on me that I won't put on myself. I'm managing the project. I'll give the presentation." Before he could respond, she went on, "You didn't say much of anything once we all started talking about the school. Why not?"

Now they'd gotten to it. He ran a hand through his hair. "We're nowhere near ready to open the school to anyone."

"Then why didn't you say that to him?"

He shrugged.

The light in her eyes dimmed as quickly as if he'd thrown a switch. "You mean you think *I'm* not ready." She shook her head. "I should have known when you assumed you'd do the presentation. You still don't think I can handle my job, do you?"

Damn. A need to touch her had him shoving his hands into his back pockets. At the same time, he had to clamp his jaws together to keep from saying something he would regret.

The dullness of her expression told him he didn't need to answer. She had read his face and already knew how he felt. He wanted to deny what she'd said but didn't have it in him. He wanted to lean down for a kiss, but he couldn't do that, either.

Most of all, more than ever, he wanted to head back home.

Chapter Thirteen

Ryan settled back against an outcropping and watched the sun start its climb over the ranch house. The reddening sky just about matched his mood. The pair of hawks circling overhead didn't help it any, either.

In the days since their supper at the Double S, Caleb hadn't said a word about sending him to Montana. He also hadn't demoted him.

And things hadn't gotten any better between him and Lianne.

He rested his head back against the rock. Tossing and turning throughout the night had left him with a crick in his neck he couldn't seem to loosen. Or maybe the stiffness had started working at him before then, the result of spending too much time around her with his hands firmly by his sides and his jaw clenched to keep from saying a whole list of things he shouldn't.

His nightmares had been pushed aside to be replaced by dreams of her. For that alone he ought to give thanks. But bad as his nights had been for months, the dreams sure as hell didn't make life any easier. Especially when, as this morning, he woke with the feeling he could give new meaning to the term *sexually frustrated*.

In desperation, he'd left the main house earlier than usual and headed out on the stallion, not even stopping at the bunkhouse. Not wanting to face Tony, who had picked just this time to go quiet on him, too.

He'd hoped a long solitary hike would clear his mind. And still his thoughts turned to Lianne.

Here on the western border of the ranch, where the hiking trail cut through the piñons and pines, everything reminded him of her. Next to him the sun-dappled stream she'd knelt beside to splash water on her face. Across from him the concrete picnic bench where he'd first kissed her. Even a look down at the sea of wildflowers and underbrush hugging the base of the mountain called to mind her bright-colored skirt flipping around her knees.

A few hundred yards beyond where he sat was the clearing she'd told him about, reached by a bridge high above the stream. He'd walked up there to take a look but didn't cross to the opposite bank. That was her quiet, beautiful place, her shrine.

Not his.

Lately they hadn't shared much of anything.

And yet, whether on foot or on horseback, it was always the same. He couldn't keep from making the familiar trek to the ranch house. Still her boss, he made a point of checking in with her regularly.

Man up and tell the truth. He made multiple trips to her office every day.

He didn't want to think about which of those visits tied in to his responsibilities as ranch manager and which were solely an excuse to see her again.

At each meeting, he could feel her reluctance to give him updates. With summer upon them and the crew taking vacation time, the construction had slowed down. She wouldn't tell him that, but he could see the rate of progress for himself.

He could see the evidence of her progress, too. She'd

begun focusing on outfitting the main building, including stocking the mess hall from dishes to nonperishable food. She claimed her job description covered everything.

What she didn't own up to was the balance she seemed to have established for their meetings, with business on one side of the scale and all else on the other. Whenever the talk started to drift over to anything other than work, she'd back off.

Well, he could understand that. He had plenty of history he didn't want to discuss, either. But he had trouble keeping his balance with those scales of hers.

Hell, he couldn't find his balance around her at all.

He wanted to resolve their conflicts to make their business relationship less rocky, but she just turned her head away whenever she wanted to tune him out.

He wanted her in his bed, but that sure wasn't happening, either.

Yet, the higher his frustration climbed and the longer he was denied satisfaction on either count, the less sure he became about which priority topped his list. About which *want* weighed more heavily on *his* scale.

Overhead, those hawks circled lazily, their effortless glide only making his own turmoil more evident by comparison.

"TROUBLE IN PARADISE." Ellamae made the flat statement, not expecting—and being darned if she'd accept—any argument from her sister.

"It did seem like Lianne and Ryan weren't altogether happy when we left," Roselynn said with some reluctance. She kept her eyes on the dough she was working on the counter. The Whistlestop had a few guests staying for the weekend, and she was going to town making all sorts of breakfast goodies.

"*Seem like? Ha.* The trouble between these two is clearer than Sidewinder Creek after the spring rains."

She couldn't understand folks sometimes. It had been nearly two weeks since their dinner at the Double S. Two long weeks, with Roselynn going around the kitchen in a huff and Tess giving her long, unfathomable looks and even the judge glowering at her in chambers. Ellamae had been fit to be tied—although that phrase didn't much apply to her.

No one could tie *her* down. Or tell her what to do. She would put her plan into action—when it was time.

Roselynn was the only holdout. Shoving aside a mixing bowl and two spatulas, she looked her sister in the eye. "Why are you dragging your heels over this, Rose? You saw those two on the dance floor. Don't tell me you didn't see sparks from *both* of them, now."

"I know, but…I just don't think we ought to get involved. Caleb won't like it."

"He'll like it a lot less if he loses a good foreman." She took another scone from the cooling rack and bit into it.

"I'm sure he's handling things."

"*Ha* again. Did you ever know a man who could handle getting two people together when they think they want to stay apart?"

"This is different. Ryan's already been through so much—"

"And it's only going to get worse without a little outside assistance at the appropriate moment." She turned her head to listen to the footsteps coming from the direction of the dining room. "Tess is on the way." She took another scone and retreated to her chair at the kitchen table.

Tess took a mug from the cabinet and a tea bag from the tin. "Aunt El, you've got that cat-who-swallowed-the-canary look."

"Not even close." She raised her plate. "I'm eating scones."

"Uh-huh." Tess swiped one herself and sat at the table. "So, what are you up to?"

"Nothing."

"Why don't I believe you?"

"'Cause your mama raised you wrong."

"El!" Roselynn protested.

The kettle whistled. Tess went to get it and filled her mug. "You're up to something." She stood holding the pot over Ellamae's mug. "Hot water?"

Darn the girl. "Not if I can stay out of it." But she pointed to the mug, and Tess tilted the kettle. "I've a funny feeling you could be helpful."

"I've just poured your tea, haven't I? And—" Tess paused and eyed her "—I've just been to visit Kayla. Lianne was there, too."

"Is that so." She looked thoughtfully at her niece. "How are the girls doing?"

"Kayla's fine but restless. Lianne seemed quieter than she usually is. We're both concerned about her."

Ellamae tried not to smile into her tea. It was time.

"Poor thing," Roselynn said. "She's got a lot on her plate with that school going up."

"Yes, and with the scouts coming in just a couple of days." Tess stared at the steam rising from her mug. "When I left Kayla's, Lianne had just mentioned bringing Becky and P.J. into town for ice cream, then taking them to the playground."

"Had she? I might just walk on over there."

"Good idea, Aunt El. I'm sure you'll be very helpful."

"As always." She winked. "You're not so bad at that yourself."

Over the rim of her mug, Tess smiled.

LIANNE KEPT HER gaze from drifting a few dozen yards away to the Flagman's Folly Community Center, but she had no control over her thoughts. They drifted to what had happened inside that building. She couldn't help but wish she and Ryan had gone to the party solely for the pleasure of each other's company. Strictly to get to know each other, as he had suggested.

She couldn't help but wish the evening hadn't turned out the way it had—after she'd gotten the texts from her family and had found him downstairs in the kitchen eating pie.

She crossed her arms on the picnic bench where Becky and P.J. sat enjoying their ice cream. Becky waved to get her attention and then pointed toward the street. Ellamae was making her way to them across the playground.

Ellamae took a seat on the bench across from her. She gave Becky a quick hug, high-fived P.J. and turned back again. "How are things going out at the ranch? You all ready for the scouts yet?"

"Yes. I finished up yesterday." She had worked hard to have everything ready for Monday. To show Ryan just what she could accomplish. Getting the cabins stocked for their arrival had kept her busier than ever, a much-needed distraction to keep her from dwelling on Ryan.

The visit with Kayla and the trip here with the kids this afternoon had been a diversion, too. And now here was Ellamae.

Lianne hadn't seen her since the dinner at the Double S. She had gotten off easy that night, with Caleb's family all around. She had managed to escape the inquisition at Kayla's the morning after the party, too. When Ellamae had shown up with Nate, who'd immediately wanted to join Becky and P.J. for the overnight, Lianne had eagerly taken off with all three kids.

Another thing she couldn't help but wish—that bringing the kids to the house for the sleepover had had a happier ending, too.

"Today was my treat to myself," she said to Ellamae. "I couldn't think of a better way to spend it than with the kids."

Liar. She could think of another enjoyable way to spend the day. He just wasn't an option for her.

Ellamae nodded as if she had read her thoughts. "Yeah. I'm taking a rare Saturday off, myself. But I wanted to let you know, I got the school on the agenda for the next meeting at Town Hall. A week from Monday."

"That's great. Your magic worked."

"Always does."

Lianne laughed. The town council meeting didn't worry her. She already knew almost everyone in town. She would manage the presentation without a problem. And that night outside the Double S, she had made it clear to Ryan *she* would be the one to handle it.

Finished with their ice cream, Becky and P.J. wiped their hands and tossed the napkins in the trash. They ran to the swings on the other side of the playground.

"Those kids have a lot of energy, don't they?" Ellamae said.

She nodded.

"Tess said she saw Kayla, and she's having trouble reining in her energy, too."

"But she knows what she has to do for the baby's sake."

"Of course." Ellamae rested her crossed arms on the table. "With her expecting, I'd guess babies are on everyone's mind."

"Yes."

"Have you thought about having kids of your own, Lianne? Someday, I mean. When you find the right guy, that is."

Slim chance of that happening, either, considering her

luck with both the man she had left behind in Chicago and the one she now lived with—temporarily. She felt herself flush. Ellamae's narrowed eyes told her she had noticed it, too. She shrugged. "I'd like to have children. Someday. But it would definitely have to be the right guy."

Chances were high her children would be deaf, too. Any man she married would have to be willing to accept the odds. Ryan...

Ryan. She held back a sigh.

What were the chances he would ever accept a deaf child of his own?

And why was she wasting time thinking about it? Thanks to his unwillingness to trust in her abilities, they would never have a future together.

"I imagine you'd want to think about having those babies soon," Ellamae said. "Especially if you plan to catch up to Kayla. She's already two ahead of you."

She forced a laugh. "No contest. Kayla will always be ahead of me."

"Well, I hope you find that guy and have that family soon. Kids bring a lot of joy into life." Ellamae shook her head. "I can't imagine ever losing a child, the way Ryan did."

Her breath caught. *"Ryan?"*

How awful. She hadn't known he'd been a father. Or that he'd ever been married.

"He hasn't mentioned anything?" Ellamae asked, as if she had read her mind again. "I probably shouldn't have slipped and told you." She shook her head. "I really feel for that boy, with what he went through."

No, he hadn't mentioned anything. Not even the night they had almost made love. He wouldn't have done that if he were still married. He wouldn't have let her take him to her bedroom.

She didn't want to sit on a playground bench and exchange gossip. But if she asked him about his child…if she asked about anything now…would he tell her? Again, what were the chances?

Everything seemed to come down to chance.

"What happened, Ellamae?"

"It was a car accident. His wife was driving. She had their boy with her. He was four then. Would've been five now. Just like P.J."

Just like P.J. And Becky.

She looked across the playground and fought the urge to run over to give them a hug.

Ryan had talked to her about Becky only after she had confronted him. She could see how uncomfortable he'd felt at being around all of the kids. Now maybe she knew why. "How awful. His son. And his wife…?"

"Neither of them survived." Ellamae shook her head. Despite the woman's tendency to ask as many questions as P.J. did, Lianne knew those were genuine tears in her eyes. "Gotta have a lot of sympathy for a man in a situation like that."

"Yes."

They both sat looking at Becky and P.J.

Lianne blinked back tears, too. Why couldn't she and Ryan be close enough now to talk about this?

Why couldn't they have a future? She didn't want to imagine one without him, but what chance did they have together? They couldn't resolve their conflicts. She couldn't work happily with anyone who micromanaged everything she did.

But none of that mattered when it came down to this. Losing a child had to be the most heart-wrenching grief a parent could suffer.

Yes, she had sympathy for Ryan. All the sympathy in the world. And chances were, she would probably never have the opportunity to tell him.

BETWEEN THE BRIGHT lights shining on a billboard highlighting the bar's name and the neon lights in the window advertising different brews, Ryan could see his destination long before he arrived at it.

When Sam Robertson had called to tell him he was meeting up with another one of the local ranchers and invited him along, he'd taken him up on the idea. He'd enjoyed meeting folks at the community center, and it was about time he saw more of Flagman's Folly. The night out couldn't have come at a better time.

Tony and the rest of the boys had gone up to Santa Fe.

Lianne had taken off somewhere that afternoon, he had no idea of her plans for the evening and he wasn't about to sit at home alone. He didn't need to spend the night thinking about her, wondering what she was doing or worrying over who she was with—the way he'd done every time she'd gone out all dressed up.

The bar was out on a back highway. Probably a convenient place for folks to meet up, a thought confirmed by the crowded parking lot.

The building was rough-hewn on the outside and not much more spiffed up inside, with uneven planked flooring beneath his feet and a few low-hanging ceiling fans above stirring yeast-scented air. His kind of down-home place.

A long, well-used bar ran the length of one side of the room, a row of booths traveled down the other and a scattering of tables filled the middle, with barely a vacant seat in the house.

Sam had staked his claim on a far booth. Ryan made his way over there, dodging the lone waitress he could see working the floor. She carried a tray loaded with mugs and bottles.

"Hey." He dropped his Stetson on the empty seat. "Think I'll go pick up a brew before I sit."

"Good idea. It'll probably be a wait otherwise."

At the bar, watching the waitress, he thought again of Lianne and the challenges she would have faced.

When he slid onto the wide leather bench across from Sam, he asked, "The place always this crowded?" He raised his voice over the conversations going on around them and a burst of laughter from the table for six near their booth. In the corner, a jukebox blasted a song into the room.

Lianne would enjoy the bass.

"They're busy here Fridays and Saturdays, yeah," Sam said. "The saloons are few and far between around Flagman's Folly, so this place gets most of the trade." He gestured with his mug. "How're things going out at the ranch?"

"Good. Caleb's back up in Montana, but we're getting things pulled together. Everything's set for the group we've got coming in Monday."

Sam nodded. "Yeah, Lianne mentioned the scouts when she was over at the house the other night."

"She's done a good job getting things together for them." He had to give her that.

"She's a phenomenal woman," Sam said, shaking his head. "Kayla's told me before how tough it is for someone profoundly deaf to do so well with lipreading. She's a great role model for Becky. For anyone, when it comes down to it."

"Yeah." He focused on raising his full mug of beer without spilling it all over the table.

Sam looked past him and raised his hand in a greeting. "Here's Ben." He slid farther across his side of the booth to make room for the newcomer.

Once the man was seated, he reached across the table.

"Ben Sawyer. Otherwise known as P.J.'s dad. I gather you two have met. He's talked up a storm about you."

And about the little boy in heaven?

He gripped his mug.

Ben Sawyer seemed as talkative as his son. Fortunately, he moved the conversation along. "The kids are all over at Sam's tonight. Which is probably why you're here, isn't it, Sam?"

The other man laughed. "I won't deny it. Kayla's climbing the walls, so my mom and Lianne thought having some friends over to visit would help distract her."

So that's where she is. He loosened his grip on the mug and leaned back against his seat. He refused to call it "sagging with relief."

"Ben's chairman of the town council," Sam said.

"Yes," Ben said, "and I'll be seeing you at the next meeting, I assume. Ellamae's sent out the agenda, and I noticed we'll be viewing a presentation about the school."

"You will," Ryan confirmed. Lianne was making good progress on that, too.

As the talk moved on to local matters, he added to it from time to time. Mostly, he let the conversation flow over and around him.

The waitress stopped by every once in a while to replace their drinks. When it came to taking the food order, she had to bend down to hear over the surrounding noise.

Sam turned to Ryan. "Did Lianne tell you she used to wait tables in college?"

"Yeah, she mentioned it." That first night she'd really talked to him. The night Caleb had made him her boss.

As he watched a few couples on the dance floor at the back of the room, he thought of the night at the community center, of dancing with Lianne in his arms. They hadn't missed a beat.

It occurred to him he could have had her in his arms to-night, the way he had at that party.

And it occurred to him, as he drove home, his night out hadn't done a thing to take his mind off her.

It wasn't that late when he got to the ranch house, but her car already sat in the driveway. It stood to reason. The kids—except for Becky, of course—would've been carted home to their beds by now. The women probably would have called it an early night anyhow so Sam's wife could get her rest.

It looked as though Lianne had turned in early, too.

The house was dark except for the lamp in the living room.

Upstairs, her door stood closed. A dim light showed beneath the door, too faint to be the overhead fixture or even the bedside lamp. Maybe the one on the dresser—that danged dresser that held that damned phone he'd allowed to destroy their one evening together.

He touched the door. Just a bare wood panel keeping him from joining her. From seeing her welcome him into her room again. But as with the phone vibrating on the dresser, she wouldn't notice his knock at the door.

He thought of opening it anyway, envisioned her eyes lighting up when she saw him and her arm sweeping away the covers on his side of the bed.

His side of the bed.

A hot rush at the thought made his body hard. Cold reality propelled that body down the hall. The certainty he'd made the right decision had him sliding into his own bed feeling virtuous for more than one reason.

It didn't have him feeling less alone.

The Louis L'Amour novel he'd carried from Montana sat on the nightstand beside him. In all these weeks, he hadn't turned a page. But it was going to be a long night.

He opened the book to the place he had marked with a scrap of paper. No…not a scrap. A picture his son had drawn. With Jan's help, and in the four-year-old's print that earned him gold stars, he had carefully labeled the stick figures.

Mommy. Daddy. Billy. Tagalong. Ocean.

Ryan closed the book and set it back in place.

The night had just gotten even longer.

Chapter Fourteen

Outside the new corral fence, Lianne stood with one of the scoutmasters, watching the boys on horseback inside it.

To tell the truth, she mostly watched Ryan at work inside the corral.

Since the scouts had arrived and started their riding lessons, he'd loosened up a bit. Maybe since the boys were closer to Nate's age than his son's, it made a difference. Maybe if the younger kids hadn't been around the other day, he would have been more relaxed with Nate, too. And maybe if he hadn't lost his son, he would have been comfortable with Becky and P.J.

Still, with the scouts, he smiled more often and even laughed with them once in a while. It had been nice to see. She wished he'd do more of that with her.

On the other hand, at the moment, he was *supervising* the other cowboys while they gave the lessons, and she wished he would do a lot less of that with her.

Busy with the boys for the past couple of days, he had backed off...somewhat. And they'd both spent more time out on the premises, together, getting along. It was probably all show for the guests, but she had to admit it had been nice, too.

The guys seem to be having fun.

Lianne nodded and smiled at Phil, the scoutmaster, who had just signed to her.

They do, she agreed, signing back without speaking. There was no need to when they could understand each other without a problem. Too bad she and Ryan couldn't do the same. She had seen Ryan watching them from time to time. It was too much to hope that overnight he had decided he wanted to learn sign language. But an interest was a start. Another step in the right direction.

Phil touched her shoulder. *Do you ride?*

She nodded.

Maybe you'll go out riding with me one day?

Ryan headed their way. She took a deep breath and smoothed her hands down her jeans.

Beside her Phil rested his arm on the top rail. When Ryan approached, he said, "Have you got— *Sorry, Lianne.*"

"Don't worry about it."

He turned back to Ryan. "Lianne and I might want to go for a ride sometime this week."

Ryan had worn a work shirt today that turned his hazel eyes blue. Now those eyes narrowed. "Thought you were here to watch over these boys."

"I am. But we've got extra supervision on this trip so we can have some time off. I've never been to the Southwest. I'd like to do some sightseeing." Phil smiled at her. *"It'll be nicer to do it with company along."*

The muscle in Ryan's jaw ticked.

She had to bite her lip to hold back a smile.

Ryan tilted his head toward the barn. "Speak to Tony. He'll get you fitted up. He's a busy man, though. Better get to him while he's around."

"Right." Phil nodded at her and then walked away.

She crossed her arms on the top rail and stared up at Ryan. ""While he's around"? Is Tony going somewhere?"

"You never know what folks will do." He tilted his head toward the barn again. "I can see the guy knows sign language."

"He took classes in high school."

"Guess he doesn't know how well you can read lips."

"He wants the practice." Now she let herself smile. "But did my eyes deceive me, Ryan? Or was that actually a compliment?"

"It's not the first one I've given you."

You're beautiful.

She swallowed hard. He'd meant a compliment about her job—he had told her more than once that she had done nice work on some spreadsheet or other—but her memory had rushed to what he'd said the night they had been in her bedroom.

She looked down, not wanting him to read anything in her eyes. "Speaking of what folks will do, thanks for getting this done in time." She touched the top rail.

He put his hand over hers. She hesitated, not looking up, wanting to stay there. For a moment. For a while. Forev—

For longer than she should. None of the scouts was near enough to see, and in any case, his body blocked their view. But she couldn't stand there out in the open in the warm sunshine under a sky as blue as Ryan's eyes...and hold hands with her boss.

FROM THE DOORWAY, Ryan surveyed the group of boys goofing off in the barn. After their first horseback ride since they'd started lessons, they needed a chance to unwind, but still...

"No slackers on this ranch," he announced.

One of the boys closest to him, a redhead with more freckles than an Appaloosa had spots, rose from his stool and saluted. "Yes, *sir.*"

"At ease, cowboy. Take a load off."

The kid grinned and sat again.

He hadn't expected to get along with the boys as well as he did. They were older, though, and that made all the difference.

He and the cowhands had put in plenty of extra work to prepare for their guests. Caleb had brought in several more horses, and they'd readied the saddles, the tack and everything else the scouts would need for their rides. Lianne had appreciated that they'd finished the corral.

The extra work had kept him away from the main house—and Lianne—but the arrival of the scouts had unexpectedly changed things in that regard, too.

A shadow spilled across the barn floor beside him. The boys' grins provided the first clue as to who'd come up to stand beside him. The faint scent of roses gave him the next.

Another benefit of having the scouts around. He got to see a lot more of Lianne.

She wore a plaid Western shirt, nice-fitting jeans—*real* nice—and the boots that had started to look a lot more lived in than when he'd first seen them on her.

He would have liked to wrap an arm around her and pull her close. *Not in front of the boys.* That was what Lianne would have said if he'd tried it. When he'd touched her hand on the corral fence, he'd seen the way she'd backed off... after a while.

It had taken her even longer to walk away when he'd brushed a flyaway strand of hair from her cheek this morning. Hell, he'd stood there for a while, too, after she'd left him.

"How's it going?" she asked.

"Not bad. Though we could use less saddle soap and a lot more elbow grease around here." He frowned at the redheaded kid, who laughed and got back to work.

"We've just brought home the food for tonight," she said. *We?*

"Need any volunteers to take it over to the cabins? These guys can probably put the good deed toward their merit badges." She wouldn't ask *him* outright for help. If he offered it unbidden, he'd no doubt get that "I can handle it" line again. He had to admit, she might be possessive about this project, but she worked darned hard for it, too. No job was beneath her, including taking care of all the food and extras they needed for tonight's campfire.

"That would be great," she said. "And…Becky and P.J. are with me, too. They wanted to come for the campfire."

He nodded grimly. He wouldn't place any bets on how many sacks of groceries they had carried.

Eyeing the redhead, as well as the two boys next to him, he tilted his head toward the door. They dropped their sponges and scrambled to their feet.

"The car's right by the house," Lianne told them.

They took off running. She followed more slowly, and he fell into step beside her.

He felt uneasy, for more than a couple of reasons.

They hadn't discussed the presentation again. Before the day came, he'd have to tell her he hadn't changed his mind. Caleb had put the responsibility of managing this ranch on his shoulders, and he wasn't about to give up an opportunity to show his boss he had a handle on things.

When he reached her car, he found Phil, the scoutmaster, leaning up against the Camry, showing off his signing skills to Becky.

"I told you boys, no slacking off," he said mildly.

The scouts loaded themselves up with grocery sacks.

"Where to?" asked the redhead.

"The mess hall, Kenny," Lianne told him.

"Forward, march," Ryan added.

The boy tried to salute and almost lost a sack.

"Good thing there aren't any eggs in there," Lianne called after him as he led his friends away.

Ryan looked at Phil, who hadn't moved from the side of Lianne's Camry. "Still on a break?" he asked in his previous mild tone.

"Not as of right now."

The guy got up, smiled at Lianne and signed something to her.

He watched them and thought of the cowboy he'd sucker punched, then shook his head. Not the way to go here. Not the way to go at all anymore.

But he couldn't help wondering, as he already had too many times to count, if Lianne had taken the guy to the trail. If she'd shown him her quiet, beautiful place. The place *he'd* had the chance to check out but hadn't set foot in without her.

Well, he'd have to take his chances on that one.

He rested against the side of the car and crossed his arms.

As Phil walked away, Lianne turned back to him. "The boys seem to be doing well."

"They're getting by," he admitted. "Two days ago some of them didn't know the back end of a horse from the front."

"They're quick studies."

He eyed her, frowning. She didn't need to spell it out. He recognized her pointed reminder of the day in her office when he'd acted like a horse's ass.

"Caleb was smart to host the scouts here now," she said. "Since they have scoutmasters along to supervise them—"

Scoutmasters…right.

"—I didn't need the counselors on-site, though they're all lined up for opening day. The cabins were ready when the scouts arrived, and—"

She hadn't raised a hand, yet he could see her counting the items off on her fingers. Making a point of her efficiency.

"—now we've got all we need for the campfire. Everything," she finished, "has worked out fine."

He couldn't resist. "Their stay's not over yet."

She shook her head. "Very funny. You have to agree, things are moving ahead of schedule. With Caleb bringing in the new horses for the scouts, we'll even be able to start riding lessons as soon as the students arrive."

He'd be long gone by then.

"Face it, Ryan. I know how to do my job."

She said the words calmly enough. But when she turned away, she marched off as if he'd given her the same order he'd jokingly given the boys. Only she moved with a lot more speed than they had—and looked a hell of a lot better in a pair of jeans.

Even as he stared after her, he rubbed his jaw and gave himself a pointed reminder. Caleb might not have said anything yet about sending him back to Montana, but that would happen. He and the boss both knew it was getting to be time.

LIANNE SAT ON the top porch step at the main school building. All afternoon she had kept a close eye on Becky and P.J. They now sat on the bottom step, helping Tony shuck ears of corn.

She had kept an equally close eye on Ryan. Since he seemed to get along better with the scouts each day, she had decided to risk bringing the kids to visit the ranch again. To give him a chance to get comfortable with them. And maybe, in some small way, to help him recover from the devastating loss of his son.

So far the plan had backfired. Ryan hadn't come anywhere near them. If not for P.J.'s habit of asking questions, the kids might not have seen him at all.

To be fair, Ryan *had* been busy most of the day with the older boys. She glanced toward the porch of the next cabin, where the scouts huddled around their troop leaders and Ryan.

Tony came out of the door just behind her, carrying another bag of corn. He stopped beside her and nodded toward his helpers. "These two don't want to get in on the action?"

"I don't want them to." She tried to keep her voice low. "The scouts are doing something over there for merit badges, and it involves sticks and string and jackknives."

"Ah. Better to keep them away, then. They could watch, though."

She shook her head. "But they wouldn't. P.J. would want to participate. And Becky would insist on doing whatever they're doing."

"Sounds like somebody I know." Grinning, Tony went down the steps.

She couldn't help smiling, too, at the thought of Becky following in her own "I can do it" footsteps. But her smile slid away as she thought of Ryan and of how much tension her need to prove herself had caused between them.

Tony squatted beside the kids and put the entire bag of corn into Becky's lap. She laughed and dug her hands into the bag.

When Ryan began walking their way, P.J. jumped up and ran toward him.

She could see P.J. chattering. Becky looked up but returned to her job of shucking corn.

Lianne had nothing to distract her from watching Ryan and P.J. They stood too far away for her to read their lips. Too far away for her liking. She wanted Ryan closer. She wanted Ryan to stay away. So typical of her lately, she struggled to decide *what* she wanted from him.

She went down the steps to lean against the railing at Becky's shoulder. Even as he approached, she still couldn't make up her mind. He stood for a moment looking at the door at the top of the steps. Looking like a man who wanted to enter the building but couldn't face having to run the gauntlet to get there.

P.J. grabbed a discarded cornhusk, plopped it on Becky's head and laughed. "Look, Ryan, Becky's a scarecrow."

Becky laughed and patted her head.

"She said 'Hat,'" P.J. explained.

Lianne watched Ryan.

He wouldn't ignore Becky now. Not with P.J. waiting for his response and Tony standing a foot away listening. Not with Becky staring straight at him.

After a moment, he smiled and said, "That's a very pretty hat."

When Lianne signed what he had said, Becky grinned.

She smiled back, feeling more elated than she should have.

Maybe her plan to help Ryan would work after all.

RYAN WATCHED THE scouts haul rocks into the clearing in front of the cabins. To show off their woodsman skills, they had taken charge of making the fire ring.

P.J. sat beside him on the cabin step.

He'd gotten used to the boy. Getting to know his personality, different from Billy's in many ways, let him relax more around him. The kid talked nearly nonstop and was funny along with it.

He still couldn't get comfortable around the girl. But with the little time he had left here, it wouldn't matter enough to make a difference.

Kenny, the redhead, was bragging to his friends about his plans to start the fire with a couple of twigs.

"Even if you can do it," one of his friends said, "it'll probably take you all night."

"Yeah," the other added, "and we've got a ton of food to cook."

"Don't worry," Ryan told them, "I've got a box of matches handy."

"Ha, ha," Kenny said, rolling his eyes.

"There's lots and lots of marshmallows, too." P.J. licked his lips. "I'm gonna eat a million-bazillion marshmallows."

Ryan laughed. Then he shook his head. It wouldn't be so funny if the kid really did overdo it and wound up sick with a stomachache all night.

He looked across the clearing to where Lianne had set up a few camp chairs. She sat talking with Phil, the scoutmaster. Scratch that—she sat *talking and laughing* with Phil, the scoutmaster.

Well, he wasn't going to haul off and do anything stupid. But all of a sudden he felt a little stomachachy himself.

Becky sat with them. A five-year-old didn't make much of a chaperone.

And how sick was it to have a thought like that? He ground his jaw and just managed to keep from spitting in the dirt in disgust at himself.

However, that didn't stop him from getting up and moseying across the clearing.

P.J. hustled along beside him. "Where we goin', Ryan?"

"To take care of business." When they reached the porch, he said to Lianne, "The fire ring will be ready soon. We need to take care of a few things."

"Of course."

Phil left to join the scouts. Lianne led the way into the cabin. P.J. and Becky followed.

"Hey, Ryan," P.J. said, "want to play checkers?"

"Maybe later." He trailed Lianne into the kitchen.

"By the way," she said, "before we get started, there's one thing I wanted to mention."

"What's that?"

"Your bad language." Her smile almost made him miss what she'd said.

He smiled back. "And what bad language would that be?"

"When Kenny dropped that rock on your foot a while ago, you said a very naughty word."

He laughed. "Hey, if a boulder landed on your toe, you'd be cussing, too. But I did it under my breath. No one else heard me."

"Ah." She nodded. "But I read lips. You're never safe around me."

He moved closer. "I could say the same about you."

Still smiling, she surveyed the counters. "I think we've got everything we need here."

"Do we?" he said, looking at her mouth.

She hesitated for a long moment and then said, "Well…I don't know. What was it you wanted to take care of?"

"You." He moved another step closer. The toes of his boots grazed hers. "I've missed you."

Her eyes widened, but she said nothing.

"You know what I'm heading for, Lianne. If you want it, too, give me a sign."

Her tongue touched her lips.

He leaned in.

She pressed back against the edge of the counter. "No. That wasn't it. That was only a reflex."

"Too late." He waited just long enough to see her lips curve.

When he bent his head, she was ready for him, her breath tickling his cheek before he caught her mouth with his. It had been a long time since he'd kissed her.

He slid his hands around her waist and urged her toward him.

She was firm beneath his fingers, soft against his chest.

And right about the time she shifted her hips beneath him and he rocked his in a reflex of his own, he realized he might have started something he couldn't control.

Chapter Fifteen

In the glow of the flames from the fire ring, he watched Lianne interact with the kids, with the scouts, even with the scoutmasters. Now her conversations with Phil didn't cause him to blink an eye.

Phil hadn't been the one in the kitchen with her.

He didn't know the source of the strength he'd found to take his hands from her hips and step away when every part of him just wanted to *take*—another taste, another touch, another minute.

He had a bad case of lust over Lianne. But damn, it felt good.

He looked at her now, laughing at a joke one of the scouts had just told, and wished he could get her alone again.

"I ate three hot dogs," P.J. informed him.

He turned to the boy. "I saw you."

"They were yu-u-um-*my*. One with ketchup. One with mustard. One with relish. I like the relish best. It's sweet."

"Yeah." So was Lianne. If he closed his eyes, he could taste her on his tongue.

"Don't go to sleep, Ryan! We still have to eat the marshmallows. And the s'mores. Do you like s'mores?"

"Yeah, I do." But not more than he liked Lianne.

He shook his head to clear it. He needed to stop thinking these thoughts or he'd never make it through the evening.

"Did you sing the songs with us? I didn't know all the words, only some."

"I'm not much of a singer," he admitted. Hell, he'd barely paid attention. He'd spent the sing-along time torn between looking at Lianne in the light on the other side of the fire ring and trying not to look Lianne's way.

Becky sat beside her. Neither of them could hear any of the words to the songs. Or any of the voices around them.

All these weeks, it hadn't mattered that Lianne couldn't hear his voice. From watching her with Caleb in the beginning, he'd learned to get her attention before he wanted to say something. To always look right at her when he spoke and to slow his speech down some, too.

He'd gotten used to the noise level around her, from the clanging file drawers to the crashing pots and pans to the booming radio. And he'd reached the point a while ago where he could understand her speech without a hitch.

Come to think of it, she'd gotten good at reading him, too. That brought a smile to his face.

Now he listened to her voice as she told the scouts a joke. Something about a deaf man and wife in a car at a motel...

He drifted away from the story and watched her instead. Her mouth as she spoke, her hands as she signed for Becky, her hair as it shifted in the firelight. He thought about a motel room for just the two of them.

"*...and when all the lights went on, only one room stayed dark. And that's how the man knew where his wife was.*"

Everyone around the circle laughed.

He might have enjoyed the joke, too, if he'd heard it all the way through. But he'd missed a lot of it.

The way Lianne sometimes missed things.

Natural when more than one person was talking at once or if the situation didn't work for lipreading. The night at the Whistlestop, she'd struggled with Nate's enthusiastic delivery. She'd gotten lost in many of the conversations at the community center.

When he was alone with her, he could make all those adjustments he'd learned. But he couldn't do anything about the times she found herself lost in a crowd. No matter how much he wanted to, he couldn't save her from the frustration of not knowing what someone had said.

Which was another reason he wanted to be the one to give the presentation at Town Hall. Besides...maybe he'd finally get the chance to make a good impression on the folks of Flagman's Folly.

LIANNE LAUGHED AS she watched P.J. and Becky. They would stretch a charbroiled marshmallow until it reached its limit and broke and then try to catch the sweet, sticky strand with their tongues.

She thought of the sweetness of Ryan's mouth against hers. Her lips still tingled from those lovely moments in the kitchen. She had known what he'd wanted. She had wanted it, too. Thank heaven he had managed to pull away and remind her of the kids in the other room, because she hadn't had a functioning brain cell left.

She'd felt his desire, as well, and the memory alone made her flush and feel grateful for the warmth of the fire to excuse any added redness in her cheeks.

From the camp chair beside her, he met her eyes.

The heat in his gaze made the flush spread upward and over her scalp. He squeezed her hand and smiled as if he knew very well what caused the color flooding her face.

She took a deep breath. "I hate to break this up," she said, "but I think it's time for me to get the kids back to the house."

"They're staying the night?"

Nodding, she watched his expression for disappointment or frustration, the sign that would show he wanted to continue what they had started in the kitchen. She looked for irritation or annoyance, an indication he didn't want to have to deal with Becky and P.J. at the ranch house again.

But she didn't read any of those emotions in his face.

He simply nodded, squeezed her hand again and smiled.

She waved to get the kids' attention. *"Come on, guys, time to go home."*

It took them a while to gather up their things, but when Becky and P.J. finally started heading toward the house, Lianne waved a quick goodbye. She smiled at Ryan and turned to follow the kids.

Not gonna happen.

Ryan rose from his camp chair. She wasn't about to get away without him. He caught up with her halfway across the dimly lit clearing.

When he touched her shoulder, she turned. Surprise and pleasure mingled in her face, and his stomach started a flip.

"You don't need to come with us," she said. "It's not that far to the bunkhouse, and we can see the lights from here. You can stay with the scouts."

He shrugged. "Everything's covered. The boys have cleanup duty, the troop leaders will handle the fire and Tony's here for the final checkup. I'm not needed."

"I wouldn't say that." She smiled.

His heart thudded. But when he took her hand, her eyes grew wary.

"The kids will be up for a while."

He nodded. "I figured that. I can handle it." He hadn't intended to quote her, but the idea made him smile.

They walked back to the house in silence—except for P.J.'s chatter and the occasional crunching of brush underfoot.

Lianne had left the light on in the kitchen. When they all went inside, the kids immediately settled at the table.

Becky curved one hand as if holding a glass, but instead of pretending to drink, she rested her thumb on the back of her other hand and rubbed it against her skin.

"Oh, no," Lianne said. *"After hot dogs and corn on the cob and s'mores and everything else? You can't possibly want hot chocolate tonight."*

Both kids made fists and shook them up and down.

Groaning, Lianne looked at him. *"That means 'yes.'"*

He nodded. "I recommend you go easy on the marsh-mallows."

She laughed.

P.J. dropped the sack of games onto the table and spilled out the contents. "Checkers, Ryan."

"Why don't you pick something you all can play."

"Chutes and Ladders!" P.J. said.

Billy's favorite board game.

He could see him at the coffee table standing on tiptoe to spin the dial, as if that would help him score the number he wanted. He could hear him screeching with laughter when Ryan hit a space forcing him to slide down a chute.

Becky put her fingertip to her cheek and twisted it.

"Candy Land," he said.

"What?" Lianne looked as if she thought she hadn't read him correctly.

Without thinking, he had blurted the name of Billy's second-favorite game. He looked from her to Becky and back again. "She wants Candy Land," he said, as if they played it together every day of the week.

Lianne looked at the table. *"It's not here."*

"We left it in the living room," P.J. said. "I'll go get it."

"How did you know?" she asked, her tone puzzled but her lips already curving in a smile.

He shrugged. "I may not be a quick study, but I catch on to things. Eventually."

ALONE IN THE KITCHEN, Ryan stacked the boxes on the table. They'd played a board-game marathon until the kids had started nodding off.

"Don't let them fool you," Lianne had said before following Becky and P.J. out to the living room. "They'll be up chatting half the night. I'll have to leave a light on downstairs."

He had nodded. They'd always kept a night-light on for Billy, too.

He frowned, thinking of that and of the joke about the man and his wife and the lights in the motel. Of walking back to the house across the dark clearing, letting the light Lianne had left on in the kitchen guide their way.

Of the night they'd gone to her room. The night they'd almost made love. She wouldn't let him turn off the lamp... and he hadn't gotten it until just now. She wouldn't let him turn off the lamp because she couldn't read his lips in the dark.

Smiling, he shook his head. *Damned idiot.*

Maybe he did catch on to things eventually, as he'd told her a while ago. But some of those things sure took him a hell of a long time to figure out.

Lianne returned and sank into her seat at the table. "I managed to get them into their sleeping bags, but I can't guarantee how long they'll stay there."

"They'll be up for drinks of water," he said automatically.

"You've had experience."

He shifted the pile of games on the table.

"It's obvious," she continued. "You knew all the rules to the games." When he said nothing, she added, "And as we reminded the kids a few times, one of the rules is taking turns. Then there's minding manners. We've talked about me. I have to be polite and give you a turn."

He took a sip of tepid chocolate.

"Tell me about him," she said softly.

Word had gotten out. Someone from Flagman's Folly had told her about his wife and son. He had known it would happen sooner or later. He was actually surprised it had taken this long. "What do you know?"

"Just that he was four and there was an accident."

He nodded. "Billy. He had a cowlick like P.J. Asked a lot of questions like him, too." At a loss, he gestured at the boxes. "Chutes and Ladders was his favorite game. We played it three or four times a week."

"Did you let him win?"

Despite the pain of the memories, he chuckled. "Hell, no. I couldn't get away with that. He wanted to win on his own."

To do everything on his own. Like Lianne.

He cleared his throat, licked his dry lips. He couldn't look at her. He wasn't sure he wanted to talk. But he thought of all the things she had told him about her school days, her rebellion. Her challenges. He ran his finger down the handle of his mug. "He didn't want the other kids to know he slept with a stuffed tiger. He thought tigers were tough, but still…"

"Did he have any pets?"

"Yeah. A pony and a parakeet. Tagalong and Ocean. We told him the bird was as blue as an ocean." *As blue as your eyes*. He tightened his hand around the mug. "Once we said that, he wouldn't hear of any other name."

"Stubborn child. Sounds like he took after you."

He laughed softly. "Maybe." He sipped again from his mug. He hadn't talked about Billy like this since it happened. Maybe he'd started to heal some. Maybe she just asked good questions.

"Did he like school?"

"Oh, yeah. He loved preschool. He'd bring home a gold star for something every day."

"He made his daddy proud, didn't he?"

His throat closed.

"What happened, Ryan?"

He breathed for a while until his throat loosened up, and then he shook his head. "An accident. My wife and son were both in the car. They went into a skid at eighty-five miles an hour, hit a concrete wall. So they tell me."

"You don't believe the reports?"

"They're not reports. They're just empty words. The speed, yeah. Skid marks, winding up against the wall, yeah. But that's all they could tell me. And there were no witnesses." He shoved the mug away from him. "You don't just go into a slide for no reason. Something had to cause it. But I don't know what happened."

When Ryan turned his head away, Lianne bit her lip, trying to focus on the pain there and not the one in her heart, knowing how much more hurtful these memories must be for him.

He had turned away without thinking, but she didn't need to see his face to know tension ran through him. She could see it in the way his shoulders had risen and in the sudden cording of the muscles in his neck.

She moved to stand behind his chair. For a moment, she just held on to his shoulders. Then she smoothed her hands across them and began to knead the tight muscles.

"I can't read your lips now, but I can read what your body's telling me."

Her hands rose and fell. He had taken a deep breath and released it.

She closed her eyes and bent to rest her forehead against his crisp hair for just a moment. It smelled of wood smoke from the fire. She took a deep breath, too. "Do you remember the day we met?"

A muscle ticked in his jaw. She'd seen that happen time

and again, and this time she longed to reach up and stroke his face, to ease his tension.

But she sensed he didn't want her to see him.

Finally, he nodded.

Unable to have a conversation with him from where she stood, she tried to ease his pain through her words alone. "When Becky ran out into the street that day, she'd gone after Pirate. She knows she's supposed to look first, but we don't always do what we're supposed to do. She chased Pirate because she wanted to protect him. She did it without thinking. Out of instinct. Because it's an instinct to take care of those you love."

He shook his head.

She caught the words on his lips only because she had seen them moments before.

"...I don't know what happened."

She squeezed his shoulders and brushed her cheek against his hair again. "You can't keep holding on to this, Ryan. It's not something you can control." She returned to the chair beside his. "Some things happen for no reason. Or for one we're not meant to know."

He met her eyes. "Like your deafness?" he asked.

She should have been ready for it. The unexpected question—the kind he asked so often, in a way no one else had ever done.

She nodded. "Even that. We've had deaf relatives in our family for generations. There's a medical cause. A genetic factor. But no one knows why one family is chosen over another to receive a specific gene. Or why one person in a family has a certain talent when no one else does. Or why lightning strikes one tree and not the next. There just are no explanations for some things. Like the accident that happened to your family."

The accident that made him want to control everything around him.

She swallowed hard. "I understand what it's like to want answers, though, and to be angry when you don't get them. Being born deaf made me angry for a long time, too."

"Why?"

Another truth only he would know.

"When my mom and dad sent me away to school, I thought it was because they wanted only perfect children like my sisters." She shrugged. "My first rebellion started early, at six years old. Once they rejected me, I rejected them, too. For years, that was another reason I didn't want to go home." She ran her hand along the edge of the table. "Later on I learned they hadn't rejected me at all. They loved me, and as I once told you, they did what they thought was best. From then on I wanted to be perfect for them. I thought, like you, if I could find a reason—the reason I'd been born deaf—I could fix it. But I couldn't fix something that was out of my control."

He said nothing, just watched her, his eyes dark and his hand tight on the coffee mug.

She realized she'd gripped the edge of the table, too. "And, eventually, Ryan, I figured out another truth. There's no need to fix something that isn't broken."

Chapter Sixteen

Ryan paced the floor in the kitchen. He didn't want to think about what Lianne had said in that very room last night.

But he wanted Lianne *there with him*.

After they had talked, Becky and P.J. had wandered in for a drink of water. They'd stayed a while, chattering away, and it wasn't until today that he'd realized Lianne hadn't missed a word of the conversation.

She hadn't let him miss anything, either. She'd told him everything Becky had said.

At the start of the second round of drinks, he had shaken his head, smiled at Lianne and run his hand down the length of her hair. Smooth as satin. Fine as silk. He wanted to see it spread out on her pillow. But he had taken a deep breath and said, "See you in the morning?"

She had smiled and nodded, her thoughts easy to read. She was happy he understood they wouldn't share her bed while the kids were there.

Frustrated as it made him, he was happy to wait for tonight instead. Hell, who cared if they made it to the bedroom or if they did anything at all. He just wanted to be with her again.

But he didn't know he'd be waiting this long.

Ten o'clock.

She'd left before noon to take the kids back home.

At the end of his day, he'd come back to an empty house. Frustrated desire gave way to concern; concern turned to worry; worry sucked him into old memories he didn't want to have anymore.

He shoved them away before they could fully form, knowing he was overreacting, the way she had said he'd done that first day on Signal Street. But he was eaten up by the things he couldn't control. By not knowing where she was, not knowing if she was safe, not being able to take charge and get answers and to make everything right.

To fix things.

He rubbed his eyes and ran his hand through his hair and walked over to the sink.

It was his turn now for a drink of water. By the time he'd taken a long, throat-soothing swig, he'd calmed down some.

When he heard the front door open and slam closed, he had no doubt who had just come home. He managed to walk down the hall and into the living room and to rest one shoulder against the stair rail. And he managed to smile, which wasn't hard to do once he saw the wide grin on Lianne's face.

Her eyes danced and she had her arms wrapped around her as if she had to keep the rest of her from dancing, too. "Kayla had the baby. Sam Junior."

"Everyone okay?"

She nodded. "They're fine. They're both fine. Look."

She reached into her bag and took out her cell phone.

On the screen, he saw a photo of her sister, Kayla, cradling a tiny blue-wrapped bundle in her arms. His throat tightened all over again, and he wished he'd brought the glass of water with him.

"They're all fine. Becky's ready to burst at being a big sister and Sam's stopping people in the hospital hallway to announce the news." She grinned.

He smiled back. He was happy for her, but somehow, standing just inches from him, she felt far away.

"We managed to get Becky into bed only an hour ago. She was overtired. After the council meeting on Monday, I'll bring her back here. That will give her grandmother some time to spend with the baby. And to take a break."

She laughed. The husky, throaty sound put her right there next to him again. Until now he hadn't realized how much his body had relaxed once he'd seen she had walked in the door, safe. But now, he found every part of him tensing up again. For a different reason.

"Meanwhile..." She drawled the word. She held up the phone and pressed a button.

The light on the screen faded to black.

Her blue eyes sparkled.

"Ryan, I need to ask you something."

Her face looked wary now. He rested his hand flat on the bed and tried not to jump to conclusions. He tried not to think this trip to her bedroom might be doomed to end like the previous one.

"The first time we were here," she continued, "my phone went off. I didn't see it, but you did. And even though we were...in the middle of something, you stopped and told me." Her eyebrows drew together. "Why did you do that?"

"Because I could hear it and see it and you couldn't."

"That's all?"

"No." He scowled. "Far as I'm concerned, people need to stop walking around like those things are surgically attached to their ears or their fingers. But still, I figured you had just as much right to answer your phone as somebody who could hear."

"Oh." She bit her bottom lip.

Damn, were those tears in her eyes? Maybe he'd done

the wrong thing, had hurt her when he'd tried to do just the opposite. "Bad move?" he asked.

She shook her head. "Good move. That's the sweetest thing any man has ever done for me. Any *hearing* man," she added, laughing.

The sound caught at him. Made him realize how much he'd come to love it.

"I wouldn't have answered the phone just then," she said, "if not for Kayla being so close to having the baby."

"Why not?"

"You know."

"Tell me."

She blushed. "Because we were just about to do then what we're about to do now."

"Nothing to stop us tonight."

"No."

Her smile made his heart pound. He slid his hand to the top of her blouse. With every button he unbuttoned, he envisioned another piece of clothing he had once seen her wear. The skirt flipping around her knees the night of the party. That ruffled blouse that brought out the blue in her eyes. The damp towel wrapped around her shower-moistened hips. The exercise gear clinging to every curve.

When all the buttons were unbuttoned, the snaps unsnapped, the zippers unzipped—his and hers—she lay beside him covered in nothing but cool, soft, smooth skin—tanned here, pale there, rosy-pink in other places.

And it was all his for the taking.

His body hardened and his palms itched and his heart thundered against his ribs at the thought of finally, *finally* getting what he'd wanted for so long…the chance to warm her all over.

He brushed his fingers across her cheek and lowered his head. She shifted against the pillow.

Oh, hell, no. If she pulled away now, if she'd changed her mind, if she sent him packing, he'd never survive.

"Turn off the lamp, please."

He froze. "The lamp. You're sure?"

"Yes, I'm sure," she whispered.

After a long moment, he reached for the switch. Who could blame him that it took three tries to find it. Or that he needed a deep, calming breath once the room had gone dark. He knew what making love without the lights on meant for her.

And he swore he'd prove, without a word, that she'd made the right decision by trusting him.

SHE HAD NEVER made love in the dark.

Before this her nights had been filled with obligations, with having to read lips and to anticipate needs in a room where the lights stayed on.

The experience hadn't prepared her for a night with Ryan.

With him she had no obligations, no expectations to meet.

When she had asked him to turn off the lamp, she had read his face. He had understood she was saying she trusted him.

And he didn't let her down.

Being unable to see disoriented her at first, but it excited her, too, in the unexpectedness of his breath on her cheek, his lips against her throat, his hands sliding over her hips to bring her closer.

In the dark, they were equal, each willing to share with the other. Wanting to give to the other. Eager to take turns.

In the dark, without vision, without sound, her pleasure came from scent, touch, taste. She sought every one of these from Ryan.

And he didn't let her down.

She loved this man.

She loved the cleft in his chin and his changeable hazel eyes. His broad shoulders and warm hands. His laugh that put creases in his cheeks.

She loved the concern in his face when she told him about her childhood. The understanding he had shown when he asked about Becky. The caring in his eyes when he talked about his son.

She loved the way he loved her, in her bed in his arms in the dark.

Chapter Seventeen

The sun was just coming up when Lianne left the house the next morning. Ryan had already gone to start his day, but she saw him astride his horse near the corral, looking over the new stock they had brought in earlier in the week. Even now, just the sight of him made her flush at the memory of how the darkness had freed her and what they had done.

By the time she reached him, he had dismounted and stood waiting. The expression on his face made her heart thump double time.

"Couldn't stay away?" he asked.

She laughed. "You wish. I've got a big day ahead of me and I wanted to get an early start." Holding up her hand, she tapped her thumb to start the list. "First I have to finalize and practice the presentation for tomorrow—"

He curled his fingers around hers. She looked up.

"I told you not to worry about that, Lianne. I'll do the presentation."

"No—"

"Yes." He dropped his hand. "I'm ranch foreman, and responsibility for the ranch comes down to me. Caleb's trusting me."

I trusted you.

"I'm still overseeing everything," he continued, "including the school. That means the presentation."

"I'm afraid it doesn't."

"It does. I've talked to Caleb about it."

Now her heart seemed to cease beating altogether. "You…*what?*" She knew she hadn't misread those words. She just couldn't believe he'd said them. She couldn't believe what they meant.

He had gone behind her back to Caleb.

After all that had happened between them last night, after what she had said and felt and believed…

Tears of frustration burned behind her eyelids, tears of hurt she wouldn't show and couldn't afford to feel. What a fool. What an idiot for beginning to believe in her dreams and forgetting cut-and-dried facts.

Even after all she had said to him, he wouldn't back off. He would never let her do her job on her own. He'd shown that all along.

She tried to ignore the tightness in her chest at the thought of the damage he'd done by going to Caleb. By destroying her credibility with her boss.

By proving trust flowed only one way between them and equality went only as far as her bed.

She took a deep breath. Giving way to emotion again wouldn't get the job done. And bottom line it was the kids who mattered. "My notes and the presentation are on my laptop. You're welcome to use them. If you have trouble understanding anything, I'll be around late this afternoon, after I'm back with the scouts."

"The scouts?" He frowned. "Where are you going?"

She gestured past the bunkhouse, past the construction site, to the western boundary and the mountain ridge. "If they don't have anything better on *their* agenda, I want to take them for a hike."

He nodded. "All right. If you set things up, let me know. I'll go along with you."

Despite the sun creeping over the horizon, she shivered with a chill. Then hot anger rushed through her. "Ryan. I can't fight you for the presentation, but I can handle taking a group of scouts on a hike. If something goes wrong and I'm not prepared for it, they will be." He would never know how much it cost her to say those words. She forced a laugh. "That's their motto, isn't it? Be Prepared."

"It won't hurt to have another adult along."

"Another? And who do you believe the other ones are? The scoutmasters? Because I know you don't include me on that list." She ran her fingers through her hair and tugged. "You act as if I can't manage without you. You always have. But I *can*." She brought both fists down for emphasis. To convince him. "I'm a grown woman and have lived on my own for years. Without your help. Without anyone's help. And I'm still alive to talk about it."

His shoulders jerked as if he'd recoiled from an impact.

Her breath caught. Her final words hung in the air between them like print on a page. She couldn't take back those last few words and wouldn't take back the rest. Instead, she inhaled slowly, pain tightening her chest again. And she waited.

He looked at her, his eyes dark and his mouth a straight line and that muscle in his jaw ticking. Ticking…

He didn't say a word. Didn't make a gesture. Didn't move at all.

Turning, she ran blindly toward the barn. She stumbled through the doorway and grabbed a set of reins hanging from a hook. Determination steadied her hands as she went through the steps she had copied from Tony.

Outside the barn again, she tightened the cinch and mounted. As if following the path of the sun, the mare turned to look toward the west.

Lianne tried to smile. Ryan might not get it, but at least the horse knew what she needed.

They trotted past the bunkhouse where the cowboys had already begun their day, past the cabins where the scouts still slept.

When they reached open land, she took the mare into a gallop, leaning into the rhythm, absorbing the movement, outrunning her thoughts and replacing them with the visuals around her.

But when she left the mare in her usual resting spot at the base of the mountain and started up the trail carved among the trees, the thoughts caught up to her again. They raced through her mind the way her horse had galloped across the ranch.

She understood Ryan now that he'd shared his past, but he still didn't understand her. Would he get it if she used words he could relate to—bridles and bits and reins and saddle blankets?

Then would he see how his doubts and resistance and need to control put restraints on her? How they set limitations she couldn't accept?

She hurried up the trail, wanting only to get to the clearing. Needing the shrine, the sunshine, the peace. The quiet.

Sunlight glared on the surface of the stream. She squinted against the brilliance. Blinked hard to clear her eyes.

She ran to the bridge, grabbed the rope railing, jogged onto the wooden slats. She paced across one. Two. Three.

Four turned traitor. Four gave way.

Before she could plant her right foot on five, four shattered beneath her.

Her left foot plunged between sturdy slat and splintered wood. Her left hand tightened on the rope rail. Her right arm flailed, seeking. Clutching. Grasping. Touching nothing but air.

DAMN, THE WOMAN would drive him crazy.

She trusted him well enough to make love with him. To let him love her in the dark. Yet she wouldn't trust him to help her, to take care of her. To watch out for her.

He turned from the corral and saw her, well beyond the cabins. She was *already* crazy, riding off alone and angry, pushing her horse so hard.

Disasters could happen...in an instant.

In the space of a breath.

He grabbed his reins and mounted.

He followed, feeling driven to ride at her heels but knowing the folly of them both traveling at breakneck speed. He'd get there. He knew where she was headed.

He just had to keep her in view.

She never paused, never veered from her destination and, even after she had dismounted, never looked back.

When she reached the shadow of the trees, he lost sight of her. Anxiety quickened his pace, pushed him into those shadows, crawled up his back.

Above him he could hear her boots slapping the ground. The sound made it easier to track her. It made him more eager to get to her side. A burst of speed, a few yards' gain, and he caught the flash of leather and denim.

She had reached the cutoff for the rope bridge and once across that would come to the clearing.

He had almost made the cutoff when he heard her boots on the bridge. Seconds later, wood cracked with the sound of a rifle blast.

Heart in his throat, he vaulted the final yard upward to within sight of the bridge.

She was trapped, her leg caught between two slats, the rotted splinters of a broken slat dangling on either side of her. She gripped the rope railing with one hand. The other flailed in space.

Nothing he could do but race toward her and say his prayers. That she could hold on. That the bridge would hold his weight. That he would get there in time.

His first prayer was answered, in spades.

She found the railing with her free hand and clutched the rope, one hand beside the other. She steadied herself, changed her left hand to an underhand grip, changed her right. She tightened her fingers and pulled herself into chin-up position—just as he'd watched her do that morning in the yard. And she freed her leg from its trap.

Prayers two and three weren't necessary.

But when she saw him standing at the bridge and started back in his direction, her expression told him he'd better ask for more help, fast.

When she halted in front of him and put her hands on her hips, she looked upset. Angry-upset. Downright furious.

She didn't look the least bit flustered or shaken.

Her struggle had seemed to happen in slow motion. It seemed to have taken hours. In real time only minutes—if not seconds—must have passed while she worked herself free.

And he anticipated her words before she opened her mouth.

"You're overreacting."

Signal Street again.

"I can't believe you followed me."

"Lianne." He took a deep breath. "You went tearing away from the house in no frame of mind to be on horseback. And look what happened."

"What?" She gestured toward the bridge. "I had a minor accident. I handled it."

No thanks to you. She could have said it but didn't. "You might have been killed."

"That's not something you can control." Her eyes shot

sparks at him. "If it had happened, I would have been the one responsible. I would have been the one not taking care of me. It's not up to you to save me. Even a child…" She swallowed hard. "When a child grows up…" She shook her head, tugged on her hair.

He opened his mouth, but she started again.

"When Billy grew up, you would have let him go off on his own. That wouldn't mean you didn't care about him. But you would have let him live his life. You would have given him his independence. You would have trusted him." Her voice broke.

"Lianne—"

"No. I don't want to talk to you. I don't want anything to do with *any* man who thinks I'm so useless I can't function without his help."

Chapter Eighteen

"What's up with Lianne?" Tony asked.

Ryan took his time rinsing the saddle sponge, squeezing the excess water out of it, shaking it off. Then he looked at the old man. "I don't know. Why?"

But he did know. She had pushed past him in a fury that morning and stalked off without giving him the chance to say another word. That was what he got for wanting to help her. That was what he got for caring that she could've broken her danged neck.

He ran the sponge over the soap and started working it onto his saddle harder than necessary, considering he never missed a cleanup after a ride.

"She came back in this morning and then tore out of here," Tony said, "*after* asking me to take care of her mare. That's not like her. Ever since she learned to tack up, she's made a point of doing it herself."

She was good at making points, all right. The day she'd met him, she had counted off on her fingers every blasted thing she'd wanted to get across to him.

She was good at wanting to do everything herself, too.

Tony sat staring at him.

He shrugged. "She was probably in a rush to get into the office, had a lot of work to take care of."

"I don't know." Tony shook his head. "She seemed all

steamed up over something. But I guess she calmed down and got done what she needed to at the house. She went off in the car before noontime."

So she didn't organize her hike with the scouts after all. He wasn't about to take on any guilt over that. He finished drying the saddle and started working the conditioner into the smooth leather.

Smooth as satin. Fine as silk.

He shoved the thought away. "Then I'd reckon she went into town to see her sister and the baby."

"Could be. Her car's still gone, though."

The news stopped his hand for a moment. Disappointment washed over him. He'd had the wild idea that maybe they could take a ride into town, go for supper, go anywhere. Just get away from the ranch and talk, the way they'd never had the chance to do.

Yeah, *wild.* As if he could erase the events of this morning. As if he could rewind his life. That hadn't worked a year ago. Why would he have a hope in hell of getting his wish now?

He finished up and put everything back where it belonged.

Last night, Lianne was where she belonged. But that hadn't lasted, had it.

And he had only himself to blame.

He left the barn, went to shower.

When he was done, she still hadn't come home. This time, he didn't feel the worry followed by the rush of fear. Probably because he felt confident about what he'd told Tony. She would be visiting at the hospital or taking care of Becky.

Finished dressing, he decided he'd not be the best company for supper with the cowhands. Instead, he would head into town to get something to eat.

The cab of the truck felt too quiet without the radio blaring. It felt lonely, too, which didn't make sense at all. He and Lianne hadn't talked much in the truck. She couldn't read his lips when he had to keep his eyes on the road.

From the corner of his eye, he would see her patting her thigh in time to the music—not hearing the words, she had told him, but picking up some of the drumbeats. Feeling the vibrations.

He'd see her tapping away on that damned cell phone. Once in a while he'd glance over, and she'd meet his eyes and smile.

And if he were really desperate for some contact, he would inhale deeply to catch the scent of her rose perfume. He thought he could smell it now but knew he was fooling himself. He'd fooled himself about a lot of things lately.

He wasn't deceiving himself about what he saw parked just down the street from the Double S. A silver Camry with Illinois plates.

Inside the café, he scanned the booths and tables. When they didn't offer anything of interest, he checked the row of swivel stools at the counter in the back. No luck there, either.

He nodded at Dori and threaded his way through the room to an empty corner booth.

She had followed. "Hello, Ryan. It's good to see you tonight." She held up a carafe. "Coffee?"

"Yes, thanks."

"I will bring you some taco chips," she promised.

The chips came delivered by way of the next customer to enter the café. Ellamae. The woman plopped the basket onto the tabletop and settled in on the bench opposite him as if they had arranged to meet for supper. She gave him a wide smile.

"I saw your truck outside," she said. "Saw Lianne's car,

too. If I'd have known you two were meeting here, I would have waited till she was ready to walk over with me."

"Walk over?"

"From the hospital, visiting Kayla and the baby. It's just up the street. That way." She gestured through the window beside them as if he'd asked for directions. "I'm having supper with the judge," she added. "But don't worry, we'll leave you two alone as soon as Lianne gets here. I'm sure you have lots to talk about."

Lianne wouldn't have supper with him if he were the last man in Flagman's Folly and all the women and kids had gone on vacation.

"Well, of course," she continued, "when I saw how pretty she looked all dressed up, I should've known she had plans for the evening."

His hand jerked. Coffee sloshed over the rim of his mug. His stomach tightened. He wanted a slug of coffee but knew his throat wouldn't cooperate.

Ellamae watched him sop up the spill with his napkin. She had picked up on his reaction. From that first night at the Whistlestop, she had picked up on his interest in Lianne before he'd acknowledged it to himself. That night, he had seen a look in her eyes he had told himself was concern. Now he saw something he felt certain was pity.

He braced himself to tell her the truth—he and Lianne had no plans. He and Lianne had nothing to talk about.

The door to the café opened. He couldn't keep from leaning a bit to one side to see past Ellamae. Not the person he'd hoped to see and, in fact, one he didn't want to see at all. But the man spotted him and headed his way, thumbs hooked onto his red suspenders.

"Well, hello there, Ryan."

The Texas twang brought him right back to Signal Street on his first day in town.

The judge took a seat beside Ellamae and looked across the booth at him. "And just how are things going for you, son?"

About as bad as they could be. He definitely didn't want to chat with the man about that, either. As the judge himself had made a production of saying, he knew everything that went on in his town.

Not quite. He hoped, anyhow, even though the judge had his best source of information sitting right next to him. Ellamae's eyes gleamed, most likely proving her eagerness to fill the man in on whatever news she had to tell.

"Things are going just fine," he said evenly.

Ellamae tilted her head and looked at him as if she thought otherwise.

The judge rested his hands on the table as if ready to pronounce his sentence. "Good. Caleb tells me you and Lianne are coming along fine, too. With the scouts and the school and all."

"Yes, we are." Except for that last "and all." But Caleb couldn't know everything that had gone on out at the ranch. If he had, he would long ago have sent his foreman packing.

"You haven't come before my bench yet, so I reckon you're keeping yourself out of trouble."

Now, *that* was a statement he didn't trust himself to answer.

"Though you remember I told you," the judge went on, "you were welcome to show up at my office anytime—as long as you came without a lawyer and brought a clean conscience with you."

"Judge." Ellamae shook her head.

The judge continued to look at him. "Since you haven't seen fit to stop by, I'm wondering if you might not be feeling as well washed as you ought."

Beneath the table, he curled his fingers into fists, trying

to steady himself and keep unwanted thoughts away. Damn, even his own father, strict enough when he'd had reason, had never made him feel this uneasy.

But he knew why. It wasn't the way the judge's blue eyes homed in on him. It wasn't Ellamae's calculating expression. It wasn't even the pressure of trying to think how he would answer the judge.

What worried him was knowing how he had responded in other situations. And realizing how heavily that knowledge had begun to weigh on his conscience.

RYAN SHOVED OPEN the door of the Double S. He'd finished his coffee, eaten a few chips and made his excuses to get away. He sure didn't want to stick around long enough to see which lucky man Lianne had gotten all dolled up for.

As he went down the sidewalk, headed toward his truck, he saw the lucky man anyway.

Phil, the scoutmaster, stood leaning against her Camry, his attention on the cell phone in his hands. His thumbs moved over the keys. As Ryan approached, he looked up.

"Took the night off?"

The man nodded. "Yeah. I'm waiting for Lianne."

"Haven't seen her." *But I damned well will.*

He nodded and kept going. The coffee he'd drunk churned in his gut. The chips he'd eaten sat like lumps of lead. The thought of the man waiting for Lianne, getting ready to have supper with her and then going who knows where with her afterward, all set him to pounding the sidewalk.

It didn't take long until he saw the sign with the big white H. He gritted his teeth and consciously slowed his pace. No sense barging in like a madman. He'd never get beyond the lobby, where a white-haired volunteer with a grandmotherly smile sat at the information desk. She would be calling for orderlies to strap him down and doctors to sedate him.

He didn't want to be sedated. He wasn't sure what he wanted, though. He just knew he needed to talk to Lianne before she arrived at the Double S and started her date with Scoutmaster Phil.

He smiled at Grandma and asked for directions to Kayla Robertson's room in the maternity ward. Third floor, left wing, four doors down.

Two doors along, his footsteps slowed again. Three doors and he came to a halt. He could see the observation window of the fourth room and the women inside it. The new mama, propped up in bed. Another grandmotherly type, sitting on a chair. And Lianne, standing beside them both. While the three women talked, Lianne and her sister signed. He watched their hands fly and their mouths move and, since the door to the room was closed, he heard nothing.

It felt like watching television with the volume off.

It felt like being deaf himself.

He wasn't sure he needed to know the topic of a conversation among three women in a hospital room roughly twenty-four hours after one of them had given birth. He didn't like the idea of going into the room and breaking up that conversation. And now he didn't want to talk to Lianne at all.

He couldn't think of what to say to her, except to beg her not to date another man.

But he thought of what she'd said about control.

He turned and went back the way he had come and waited for the elevator.

Now that momentum wasn't pushing him, he had time to realize where he stood. Panic rushed through him. He hadn't been in a hospital since he'd faced that sad-eyed surgeon.

At the first floor, the doors slid open. Before he could move, a man stepped inside.

"Ryan." Sam Robertson grinned at him. "Come see my son." He pushed the button for the third floor, and the doors slid closed again.

Sam didn't ask what he was doing in the hospital. He was too pumped up about his boy, listing all the information a proud daddy wanted to share. Name. Inches. Pounds and ounces. Date and time. A full head of hair and the proper number of fingers and toes.

Ryan nodded, taking everything in, automatically pairing every detail with one of his own.

"He's in the nursery right now," Sam informed him, "but he'll go in with Kayla again soon to stay the night."

Once off the elevator, they took the right wing, away from the hallway he had walked down before. His steps slowed. He lagged behind Sam.

He didn't want to look into the room filled with tiny blanket-wrapped babies or to remember the thrill of finding the crib that held his son.

He didn't want to believe he would never see Billy or Jan again.

He didn't want to accept that he had lost his family and there was nothing he could do to bring them back.

Chapter Nineteen

Ryan shook hands with so many people before the start of the council meeting, he lost track.

"Well, Mr. Molloy," said a man's voice behind him. He turned to see the judge smiling at him. "I knew I'd see you in my courtroom eventually, one way or another."

Ellamae came up to them. "Where's Lianne?" she asked him in wide-eyed innocence.

"She'll be along," he said. Or so he hoped. He hadn't seen her all day.

Last night he'd gone to bed early. He didn't want to know what time she got home from her date.

Today he couldn't keep from stopping in at the house from time to time to look for her. But with the scouts gone and her sister and the new baby sent home from the hospital, it didn't surprise him not to see her on the ranch at all.

"Well, look who's here," Ellamae said. Her tone held about as much innocence as her expression.

He followed her gaze. Lianne stood with Caleb and Tess just inside the doorway.

His heart gave a dull thud as he started toward them.

Lianne looked across the room and met his gaze. She said something to Tess, and the two women moved away. Forcing himself not to falter, he walked up to Caleb.

Ben Sawyer joined them. "Just letting you know you're last up for the evening."

"No problem," Ryan said, glad Caleb couldn't know how close he'd come to showing up unprepared. Too eager to see Lianne again, he'd gone halfway out the door before remembering her laptop and the notes she had made for the presentation.

The pounding of a gavel sounded, Ben called the meeting to order and those folks not already seated filed into the courtroom benches.

He saw Lianne slip into a seat beside Tess. He quickly headed in that direction to take the last space in the row. She had done a good job of avoiding him and they weren't in a position to talk now, but he could at least have the pleasure of sitting next to her and smelling her perfume.

She had done a thorough job with the prep work for the presentation, too, laying out facts and figures, providing info about the school and its curriculum, and explaining the employment opportunities and revenue the ranch would provide for the residents of Flagman's Folly. A damned thorough job.

She had also taken the task beyond what Caleb had first laid out, including inviting a couple of the counselors they'd hired to come talk with folks after the meeting. And during the week before the official opening date, she had scheduled an open house for the townsfolk to tour the school.

She was more than just a pencil pusher. He smiled at the thought, recalling the time she had used her pencil to curl a strand of her hair and had left that smudge on her face.

Along with her business background, she was a people person, too. He gave her credit for finding that balance. He gave her credit for a lot of things, although he'd never said so to her.

As the meeting wore on, he kept half an ear on the activity. Beside him Lianne sat leaning slightly forward. Her hair tumbled over her shoulders and down her back. Smooth and silky and tempting. But he managed to keep his hands to himself. She wouldn't want him touching her. Or doing anything else.

He had thought she was crazy for going off by herself, riding angry and at breakneck speed. And it was a crazy act, setting her up for the possibility of injury to herself or her mount. But when it came to an actual danger, when it came to watching her free her leg and walk off the bridge, she had been right all along. She *could* take care of herself.

All day long the last words she had said to him yesterday morning had rung in his head.

I don't want anything to do with any man who thinks I'm so useless I can't function without his help.

He would like to tell her he hadn't thought that—not for a minute. But how could she believe him when that was exactly how he'd behaved? Not intentionally, not even realizing it until she had made her point.

Late as usual, he finally got it.

He looked at Lianne, so close beside him and yet so damned far away. And he knew he wouldn't have to lose her to an accident the way he had lost his family. He was going to lose her because she couldn't deal with a man who wanted to control her life.

WHEN BEN SAWYER announced the presentation as the final item on the night's agenda, Lianne sagged on the bench in relief.

She had struggled not to look at Ryan, not to turn toward him, not to lean into him, not to breathe deeply enough to smell the aftershave scenting his freshly shaven jaw. Not to engage any of her senses.

But she couldn't avoid feeling the heat of him, and it was

almost more than she could bear. When they had made love, he had told her he wanted to warm her all over. He'd done that then with his hands and mouth and body. He did it now simply by being by her side.

She had wanted to forget him, had tried hard to put him out of her mind. She had buried herself in work, dated other men, spent as much time as she could away from the ranch. None of it had taken him from her thoughts.

Beside her now, he rose to go up to the front of the room. She felt an instant chill from the loss of his presence, but a chill she needed to remind her of all the reasons they couldn't be together.

Her heart went out to him over the loss of his family. She had wanted to help him, to make things better, to take his pain away. But just as she couldn't fix being deaf, she couldn't fix this for him. She wasn't broken. And he still needed to work through his grief.

It had taken her years to learn what she had tried to tell him. *Some things happen for no reason.*

No matter how much she had wanted those words to help him, they *were* only words. Empty words, as he had said about the accident report. He would have to find the truth in them—to find his own reality—himself.

Her reality had been accepting the love of her family and fighting for a place in both her worlds, hearing and deaf.

His would be to accept that his questions might never be answered. And with that acceptance, finally, to find the strength to overcome his loss.

He stood at the front of the room with her folder of notes and her laptop on the table. The distance between her and that table had given her trouble reading the council members.

She could read Ryan's lips more easily because she knew them and loved them.

That was a new reality for her to face now, too.

She loved him. She sympathized with him. She understood him. Seeing his struggle made her understand why he felt the need to control everything around him, why he wouldn't trust in her ability to take care of herself. But understanding him was one thing, accepting that control something else.

At the table, he set the laptop and the unopened file folder of notes aside. After all her hard work, all her preparation, he wasn't going to use her material. A week ago, a day ago, she would have felt angry. Incensed. Now she felt only sad.

Blinking, she tried to focus on reading him.

"I'm sure you folks in Flagman's Folly will be proud to have this school in your town," he said. "I know I'm proud to be associated with it. But I can't take credit for the idea—much as I would like to." He looked around the room, and she could see people returning his smile. "Instead, let me introduce you to the person who does deserve the credit, who's done most of the work for this endeavor and who's here tonight to tell you all about it. That's the manager of this project, Lianne Ward."

Now she saw everyone around her applauding. She saw Ryan's wry smile, this time just for her.

He returned to stand at the end of the row.

She sat, too stunned to move.

With a small bow to her, he made a sweeping gesture toward the table.

Her heart pounded and her hands trembled and her breath fluttered in her chest. She knew what he had done. His wry smile offered an apology, and his gesture turned control of the presentation over to her. She didn't think she could ever love him any more than she did right now.

The strained look around his eyes said he thought she

hadn't moved because she felt uneasy about speaking to the crowd. Yet he didn't return to the front of the room.

Instead, he smiled, pointed to her and brought his fists down in front of him.

You can.

HE THOUGHT THE evening would never end, and he wanted it to, soon, only because he would finally get Lianne alone again.

He sat through her entire presentation and then afterward when she took questions from the crowd. And the folks of Flagman's Folly were one heck of a chatty bunch.

He stood through more introductions to townsfolk, then conversations with the counselors she had hired.

He agonized through another endless span of time while she circled the room to say her goodbyes.

And he heard her praises sung by everyone who came near him. Tess and Caleb. Ben and his wife. Sam Robertson, who had attended the meeting alone and made his good news the first item on the evening's agenda. Roselynn and Ellamae, who looked at him with expressions of teary-eyed happiness and smug satisfaction, respectively. And last but not least, Judge Baylor, who had taken to acting as host for the evening.

Needless to say, it was late by the time they left Town Hall. The air had grown heavy, and from far away came the rumble of thunder. He had heard thunderstorms in New Mexico could be both vicious and deadly and hoped this one would pass them by.

He followed the Camry out to the ranch. Distant lightning flashed and crackled. If he were a superstitious man, the sight and sound would have given him bad vibes.

As it was, with every mile they traveled, he felt his spirits plunge further. Lianne hadn't looked his way once after the presentation, hadn't made eye contact with him during it and, worst of all, hadn't even blinked an eye when he'd tried to make his apology and to give her his support.

She was so good at reading folks, she had to have read him. Her lack of response made him think she wasn't interested in what he had to offer. And he couldn't blame her.

Too little, too late.

That didn't let him off the hook for other things he needed to say.

By the time they arrived back at the house, jagged streaks of lightning flashed in the sky past the western ridge and thunder followed, close enough to indicate the bad weather was on its way.

At the back porch steps, she stopped and moved aside. "I'm going to sit out here a while."

He thought of what she had told him that day they had hiked the trail. She loved thunder and lightning. He smiled. "I'll join you."

He hung his Stetson from the railing and went with her to the wooden lawn chairs beside the house. He took the chair facing the back porch light fixture. The glow turned her hair to liquid silver and partly hid her face in shadow. Lightning illuminated her fully from time to time, but not long enough for him to gauge her expression.

He sat with his fingers clamped to his knees and his heart thudding like a pile driver. He didn't know where to start or what to say. His hand itched to make a silvery slide down the length of her hair. Instead, he touched her shoulder. She turned his way.

"I talked to Sam tonight," he said. "He's still bragging about his son."

"He hasn't stopped since the baby arrived."

"Yeah. I told you Billy was my pride, too." He sighed. "But, Lianne, when I talked about the accident, I never said anything about what came after. When I couldn't get anyone to explain what happened." She needed to read his lips. He couldn't look away. But he couldn't meet her eyes.

He looked into the distance at the flashes of jagged light. "I wanted to find answers. A reason for the accident. And that need spread to everything I did."

He told her about those first weeks, when he had walked around trying to get his job done but feeling as if he moved through a fog. About the months after that, when his fuse got shorter and his temper got hotter. "But I still couldn't get answers to my questions. That wasn't something I could control. Instead, I started trying to control everything around me."

He told her about letting his frustration drive him, making him drive his wranglers, running them all into the ground so he wouldn't have to face his empty house and the long hours of not knowing.

Beyond her, lightning flashed. He waited for the rumble of thunder. Waited for the sound to die away.

Then he told her the worst. That last week in Montana, when he'd sucker punched a drunken cowboy. When Caleb had given him the news about sending him to New Mexico.

He clenched his fists, rapped his knuckles against his knees. Talking with her about Billy the other night had felt natural. Necessary. Right. What he had to tell her now was necessary, too, but not natural to him. Not at all. "When Jan and Billy died, it felt like part of me went, too."

She reached out to touch one of his fists. He turned his hand palm up and held her fingers, lightly but in the same underhand grip she had used to clutch the rope railing of the bridge.

"The part of me that was left didn't want to come here, didn't care what happened anymore. The only thing that kept me going was the thought of fixing things again."

He met her eyes. "'Things' weren't broken. *I* was. I hurt and needed to heal." He tried to smile. "But I didn't know that then. And as fate would have it, right when I most needed to fix something, you came along."

"And as fate would have it, the last thing I wanted was someone who thought I needed to be fixed." Her smile looked as sad as his had been.

"Tell me."

"I had said to you once before I couldn't fix being deaf, because I wasn't broken. But that's what some people think, no matter where I go. Either I'm too hearing to associate with the Deaf community, or I'm too deaf to make it in the hearing world." She tried to smile again. "No matter what anyone thinks, I feel comfortable in both. Together, the two sides of me make me whole. But just lately I'd started to doubt myself." Her eyes looked troubled, her face drawn. "I was trying to get that belief back again, and I couldn't take any doubts from you."

And he'd done everything wrong.

How could he explain?

Lightning crackled, illuminating the yard. Thunder boomed directly overhead.

She put her hand on her chest.

"You felt that?"

She nodded. "As if everything inside me shook. Did you feel it, too?"

"That same feeling, yes. But not right now. I felt it when you were on that bridge yesterday morning. I'll admit, at first, finding out you were deaf played some part in why I wanted to watch over you. But that hasn't been true for a long while. And it sure wasn't true then. I was angry— damned angry—when you took off. I followed you because I wanted to look out for you. But *I* was the helpless one. When I saw you on that bridge—" he gestured with his free hand "—everything inside me shook. And that has nothing to do with what happened in Montana or with you being deaf. Nothing to do with anything but how I feel about you." He ran his finger down her cheek. "I can't help wanting to keep you safe, Lianne. My instincts make me want to take care of you."

"Why?"

He smiled. "You know why. You told me yourself. It's instinct to take care of those you love." She said nothing. He felt that vibration inside him again.

Too little, too late.

But he wouldn't give up. "I don't want to fix you. I don't want to control you—or anyone." He rubbed his thumb across her fingers and then brought her hand up to kiss her palm. No fist now. No fighting him. He smiled. "I'm done fighting you, too. From now on I just want to love you."

She stared at him, that unblinking gaze that seemed to see right into him. And she shook her head. "Two halves," she said slowly, "don't *always* make a whole."

He frowned. "You're saying because you're deaf and I can hear, that's enough to keep us from being together? I don't agree with that."

"We're two different halves. We can get by without each other."

"We can. But I say we don't have to, if we want to work things out. If we love each other. What do you say?"

He waited.

Lightning flashed, already moving into the distance. Directly above them thunder gave a loud, menacing roll.

She rested her fingertips on her chest, but he didn't reach to cover her hand with his. Everything inside him shook, but he didn't feel the need to take control.

He waited again.

She stared him down, the way she'd done so many times before. "What exactly are you offering?"

"Me. Marriage. Family."

"Children?"

"Yeah." He swallowed hard. "You'll have to take my word for it when I say I'm great with kids."

"I believe you. But you remember what I told you about my family history? There's a good chance our children would be born deaf. Are you willing to take that risk?"

He smiled, brushed his thumb across her temple and kissed away the tear on her cheek. "Yeah," he said, finally, "I can handle it."

She laughed, low and soft, that throaty sound he would always love.

* * * * *

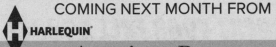
#1485 HER RANCHER RESCUER
Donna Alward

Businessman-turned-rancher Jack Shepard's been burned before. He'll be damned if he'll let vivacious Amy Wilson past his defenses! Except beneath the bubbly exterior lies a beautiful, warmhearted woman he can't resist....

#1486 HER SECRET COWBOY
The Cash Brothers
Marin Thomas

Marsha Bugler is back in Arizona asking Will Cash to be a father to a son he's never met. This time, he's determined to prove he can be the man Marsha and his son need.

#1487 BLAME IT ON THE RODEO
Amanda Renee

Lexi Lawson has kept a secret locked in her heart for fourteen years. And because of Shane Langtry's recently opened rodeo school it's about to come out, whether she wants it to or not.

#1488 SECOND CHANCE FAMILY
Fatherhood
Leigh Duncan

With her son on the verge of expulsion and a baby on her hip, young widow Courtney Smith is desperate for help. Will it come from Travis Oak, the attractive PE teacher at her son's school?

HARCNM0114

REQUEST YOUR FREE BOOKS!
2 FREE NOVELS PLUS 2 FREE GIFTS!

HARLEQUIN®

American ★ Romance®

LOVE, HOME & HAPPINESS

YES! Please send me 2 FREE Harlequin® American Romance® novels and my 2 FREE gifts (gifts are worth about $10). After receiving them, if I don't wish to receive any more books, I can return the shipping statement marked "cancel." If I don't cancel, I will receive 4 brand-new novels every month and be billed just $4.74 per book in the U.S. or $5.24 per book in Canada. That's a savings of at least 14% off the cover price! It's quite a bargain! Shipping and handling is just 50¢ per book in the U.S. and 75¢ per book in Canada.* I understand that accepting the 2 free books and gifts places me under no obligation to buy anything. I can always return a shipment and cancel at any time. Even if I never buy another book, the two free books and gifts are mine to keep forever.

154/354 HDN F4YN

Name _____ (PLEASE PRINT) _____

Address _____ Apt. #

City _____ State/Prov. _____ Zip/Postal Code

Signature (if under 18, a parent or guardian must sign)

Mail to the **Harlequin® Reader Service:**
IN U.S.A.: P.O. Box 1867, Buffalo, NY 14240-1867
IN CANADA: P.O. Box 609, Fort Erie, Ontario L2A 5X3

Want to try two free books from another line?
Call 1-800-873-8635 or visit www.ReaderService.com.

* Terms and prices subject to change without notice. Prices do not include applicable taxes. Sales tax applicable in N.Y. Canadian residents will be charged applicable taxes. Offer not valid in Quebec. This offer is limited to one order per household. Not valid for current subscribers to Harlequin American Romance books. All orders subject to credit approval. Credit or debit balances in a customer's account(s) may be offset by any other outstanding balance owed by or to the customer. Please allow 4 to 6 weeks for delivery. Offer available while quantities last.

Your Privacy—The Harlequin® Reader Service is committed to protecting your privacy. Our Privacy Policy is available online at www.ReaderService.com or upon request from the Harlequin Reader Service.

We make a portion of our mailing list available to reputable third parties that offer products we believe may interest you. If you prefer that we not exchange your name with third parties, or if you wish to clarify or modify your communication preferences, please visit us at www.ReaderService.com/consumerschoice or write to us at Harlequin Reader Service Preference Service, P.O. Box 9062, Buffalo, NY 14269. Include your complete name and address.

HAR13R

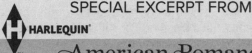
Will Cash pulled off the road and parked next to the mailbox at the entrance to the family farm. As usual the box was stuffed. He gathered the envelopes and hopped into the truck, then directed the air vents toward his face. Normal highs for June were in the low nineties, but today's temperature hovered near one hundred, promising a long hot summer for southwest Arizona.

He sifted through the pile. Grocery store ads, business flyers, electric bill. His fingers froze on a letter addressed to Willie Nelson Cash. He didn't recognize the feminine script and there was no return address. Before he could examine the envelope further, his cell phone rang.

"Hold your horses, Porter. I'll be there in a minute." Wednesday night was poker night, and his brothers and brother-in-law were waiting for him in the bunkhouse. If not for the weekly card game, they'd hardly see each other.

He tossed the mail aside and drove on. After parking in the yard, he walked over to the bunkhouse, opening the letter addressed to him. When he removed the note inside, a photo fell out and landed on his boot. He snatched it off the ground and stared at the image.

What the heck?

Dear Will… He read a few more lines, but the words blurred and a loud buzzing filled his ears. The kid in the picture was named Ryan and he was fourteen years old.

Slowly Will's eyes focused and he studied the photo. The young man had the same brownish-blond hair as Will did, but his eyes weren't brown—they were blue like his mother's.

"Buck!" he shouted. "Get your butt out here right now!"

When Buck came out, the rest of the Cash brothers and their brother-in-law, Gavin, followed.

"What's wrong?" Johnny's blue eyes darkened with concern.

Will ignored his eldest brother and waved the letter at Buck. "You knew all along."

Buck stepped forward. "Knew what?"

"Remember Marsha Bugler?"

"Sure. Why?"

"She said you'd vouch for her that she's telling the truth."

His brother's eye twitched—a sure sign of guilt. "The truth about what?"

"That after I got her pregnant, she kept the baby."

The color drained from Buck's face.

The tenuous hold Will had on his temper broke. "You've kept in touch with Marsha since high school. How the hell could you not tell me that I had a son!"

Look for HER SECRET COWBOY,
the next exciting title in The Cash Brothers *miniseries,*
next month from Marin Thomas

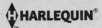
⁂American ⁂Romance®

Can't get enough of those
Cadence Creek Cowboys?

Coming soon from
New York Times bestselling author

Donna Alward

HER RANCHER RESCUER

Businessman-turned-rancher Jack Shepard's been burned
before. He'll be damned if he'll let vivacious Amy Wilson
past his defenses! Except beneath the bubbly exterior lies a
beautiful, warmhearted woman he can't resist....

Available February 2014, from
Harlequin American Romance

Wherever books and ebooks are sold!

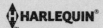
HARLEQUIN®

American Romance®

This Cowboy is About to Get Thrown

Ever since he broke Lexi Lawson's heart, Shane Langtry
has had just one true love: rodeo. The handsome cowboy
lives and breathes for competing in the ring—and for the
rodeo school he's just launched. It's more than awkward,
now that Lexi is the veterinarian who cares for the
Langtry horses. But the two do their best to get along.

That is, until Lexi is forced to reveal a secret that changes
everything. Shane can't deny that he's still drawn to Lexi.
But will this news ruin any chance of rekindling their
long-ago love?

Don't miss
Blame It On The Rodeo

by AMANDA RENEE

Available February 2014, from
Harlequin® American Romance®
wherever books and ebooks are sold.